# Resistance

# Resistance

Regina McIntyre

**To order additional copies of this book, contact:**
Xlibris
844-714-8691
www.Xlibris.com
Orders@Xlibris.com
840558

# CONTENTS

References .................................................................................................vii
Author's Note ..........................................................................................ix
Introduction ............................................................................................xi
Proloque ...............................................................................................xiii

Chapter 1 ....................................................................................................1
Chapter 2 ....................................................................................................4
Chapter 3 ....................................................................................................9
Chapter 4 ..................................................................................................13
Chapter 5 ..................................................................................................18
Chapter 6 ..................................................................................................23
Chapter 7 ..................................................................................................28
Chapter 8 ..................................................................................................33
Chapter 9 ..................................................................................................36
Chapter 10 ...............................................................................................40
Chapter 11 ...............................................................................................44
Chapter 12 ...............................................................................................47
Chapter 13 ...............................................................................................50
Chapter 14 ...............................................................................................54
Chapter 15 ...............................................................................................59
Chapter 16 ...............................................................................................63
Chapter 17 ...............................................................................................68
Chapter 18 ...............................................................................................70
Chapter 19 ...............................................................................................73
Chapter 20 ...............................................................................................77
Chapter 21 ...............................................................................................80
Chapter 22 ...............................................................................................83

Chapter 23 ......................................................................86

Chapter 24 ......................................................................91

Chapter 25 ......................................................................96

Chapter 26 ....................................................................103

Chapter 27 ....................................................................108

Chapter 28 ....................................................................112

Chapter 29 ....................................................................116

Chapter 30 ....................................................................120

Chapter 31 ....................................................................123

Chapter 32 ....................................................................127

Chapter 33 ....................................................................130

Chapter 34 ....................................................................133

Chapter 35 ....................................................................137

Chapter 36 ....................................................................140

Chapter 37 ....................................................................143

Chapter 38 ....................................................................147

Chapter 39 ....................................................................151

Chapter 40 ....................................................................154

Chapter 41 ....................................................................159

Chapter 42 ....................................................................162

Chapter 43 ....................................................................167

Chapter 44 ....................................................................172

Chapter 45 ....................................................................176

Chapter 46 ....................................................................180

Chapter 47 ....................................................................185

Chapter 48 ....................................................................188

Chapter 49 ....................................................................192

Chapter 50 ....................................................................195

Chapter 51 ....................................................................199

Chapter 52 ....................................................................202

Chapter Referrences ......................................................207

# REFERENCES

A work of fiction, based on historical events that took place in Poland during World War II.

Museum of Tolerance Multimedia Learning Center, Simon Wiesenthal Plaza, 9786 Pico Blvd. Los Angeles, CA 90035

BLOODLANDS, Timothy Snyder, Basic Books, 387 Park Avenue South, New York, NY 10016-8810

RISING 44: The Battle for Warsaw by Norman Davies, 2004, Penguin Group, 375 Hudson Street, New York, NY 10014

FIGHTING WARSAW, Stefan Korbonski, 2004, Hippocrene Books, Inc., 171 Madison Avenue, New York, NY 10016

NOWAK: Courier from Warsaw, Jan Nowak, 1982, Wayne State University Press, Detroit, Michigan, 48202

THE SECRET ARMY: The Memoirs of General Bor Komorowski, 2011, Tadeusz Bor-Komorowski, Pen & Sword, Limited, 47 Church Street, Barnsley, S. Yorkshire 270 2AS

THE SECOND WORLD WAR: A Complete History, Martin Gilbert, 1989, Henry Holt and Company, Inc., 115 West 18<sup>th</sup> Street, New York, NY 10011

WIKIPEDIA The Free Encyclopedia, Wikimedia Foundation, Inc. www.wikipedia.org

# AUTHOR'S NOTE

Resistance is a work of fiction based on the events that took place in Warsaw during World War II. Names of the important leaders and historical data of the time are used as a foundation and scaffold to build the structure of the story.

All other characters and events are purely fictional, and no reference is intended to any person living or dead.

Colonel Lansing had been in Belgium and France twenty years before and had tried not to think what he knew—that war is treachery and hatred, the muddling of incompetent generals, and the torture and killing and sickness and tiredness, until at last it is over, and nothing has changed except for new weapons and new hatreds. He was not expected to question or think, but only to carry out orders; and he tried to put aside the memories of the other wars and the certainty that this one would be the same. This one will be different, he said to himself fifty times a day; this one will be different.

The Moon is Down—John Steinbeck, 1942

# INTRODUCTION

Lt. Col. Leopold Okulicki was on desk duty at government headquarters in Warsaw the night of 31 August 1939. He was besieged by incoming telegrams from front-line units of the Polish Army. The messages continued to be tapped out in response to the latest area under attack by invading forces coming out of the west. The German Luftwaffe was discharging incendiary bombs from the sky while their army, the Wehrmacht, stormed the ground with heavy artillery and the latest in armored tanks. It would come to be known as a *'blitzkrieg.'* The Red Army of the Soviet Union assaulted the Poles from the east, on their way to unite with the Germans in accordance with the Nazi-Soviet Pact, which was signed and dated 23 August 1939.

The Polish Army made a valiant effort to ward off the attack, but they were outweighed in machinery, munitions, and manpower. By 14 September, the invading forces had them surrounded. There was no way out.

A cornered rat turns vicious, and the citizens of Warsaw reacted accordingly. Men and women, from all walks of life, joined in as partisans to destroy the vital communication systems and industrial sites. There was no separation of age or station. Aristocrats and the elite plodded alongside the working population to disrupt the functions and infra-structure that a community depends on. Every vehicle available was used to blockade the streets. Trolley cars were overturned, and fires were set in strategic areas. The invincible German tanks, which tore through the open country of the farmlands of Poland, were unable to navigate through the city of Warsaw. Many of the stalled vehicles were set ablaze by citizens who dashed into the streets to toss burning oil-soaked rags beneath the tanks. Like victims of birds of prey, the victorious, well-equipped members of the Wehrmacht, were shot down by snipers who hid behind structures and discharged a volley of bullets.

The final defeat of Poland took place in a marshy area of the Bug River. The document of surrender was signed 6 October 1939. The Poles never accepted the term "unconditional."

*Lebensraum,* German for habitat or living space, was Hitler's Master Plan for his conquered countries. The most fertile lands would be colonized with ethnic Germans. The area that contained Western Ukraine and the major cities of Warsaw, Crakow, and Lvov, was set apart. The land was suitable for good farming, and it was located just across the German border. The indigenous Polish population was compressed within the fifty-five-thousand-mile territory that the Germans labeled, the "General Government." The *Lebensraum* proposal would take fifteen to twenty years to accomplish. Twelve million Poles living in the territory would be eliminated. Four to five million Aryans of the Master Race would replace the current Polish and Jewish population. The systematic eradication of the inhabitants would be accomplished by several processes. Thousands would be deported to Western Siberia. The Nazi death camps would provide for the extermination of thousands more. Forced labor, either within the General Government, or in Germany, would eliminate an even greater amount; few captive workers survived the ordeal. Round-up shootings of innocent victims became a regular occurrence throughout the region. Had the Nazis won the war, the population that survived would become captive serfs for the Germans who had conquered their land. The man designated to put this plan in motion was Hans Frank, Hitler's personal legal advisor, who was appointed Governor General of this region in October of 1939.

# PROLOQUE

Olaf Ehrlich, read the latest quota mandate from Governor General Frank. He flung it on the desk and stared at the filing cabinets in front of him. The demand for produce to supply the Wehrmacht had intensified since Stalingrad. Easy for Frank to mandate from his lofty seat in the General Government in Cracow; he didn't have to deal with stupid, obstinate peasants.

The motto of the Peasant Battalion of the underground was, "As little, as late, as inferior as possible."

Ehrlich had given this issue his best effort. He had stepped up his retribution campaign to more brutal attacks on the farmers within his sector. Ironically, the killing and maiming of peasants seemed to bring on even more resistance. What kind of people were these? He would have to come up with a better method of persuasion in order to render the farmers compliant.

One of the most defiant farmers of Grojek, Antosh Wyzek, had recently been severely beaten for non-compliance, to the extent that he was left incapacitated and unable to perform his duties. His wife and two daughters, both under the age of twelve, tried to resume his chores. They were not meeting quota.

Ehrlich's driver parked the truck on the driveway of the Wyzek farm. Ehrlich hopped out of the passenger seat; six men jumped out of the back of the truck. The family was still at breakfast when the "collectors" broke into the kitchen armed with pistols.

"Bleiben sie!" Ehrlich commanded. "Stay!"

Teresa, the youngest, rose from her seat to find safety in the arms of her mother.

"Sitzen!" cried one of the men, as he grabbed her by the neck and flung her back on her seat.

Her mother screamed. Her older sister cowered under his glare.

Wyzek struggled in an attempt to rise from his seat.

Two of the men pulled his wife out of her chair, another pair grabbed the two girls and pushed them toward the door.

Wyzek shouted out pleas to stop the horrible action. He physically tried to intercede, but he could not move from the improvised wheel chair he occupied.

He continued to struggle into action while two of the men wheeled his chair out of the kitchen and onto the bumpy farm road. Four other "collectors" dragged his wife and children in the direction of the barn. Wyzek, strapped to his chair, continued to scream in protest. His wife tried to squirm loose in a valiant effort to rush to the girls. She was hit on the back of the head with the butt of a rifle and dragged the rest of the way by her feet. Terrified, the two girls offered no resistance.

Once inside the barn, the three of them were dropped to the floor. They were bound with rope at the hands, feet, and knees. They were not gagged. The girls' screams were deafening. Wyzek dropped his head; his chest heaved under his uncontrollable sobbing.

Cans of petrol were carried into the loft by two of the collectors. The petrol was poured about on the straw. Each man threw a lighted match, and then scrambled down the ladder. It was a gusty day—the winds coming in from the northeast.

The blaze lit up the skies and the Wyzek family's screams could be heard throughout the surrounding farms.

The Nazi's tactic of inflicting retribution while decreasing the basic survival needs of the people served to galvanize the Poles. The people united under a common cause, "Independence or Death." By the time the Warsaw Ghetto was demolished, and the Jews annihilated, the Poles realized that it was only a matter of time. They had come to understand the meaning of Hitler's *Lebensraum*.

# CHAPTER 1

The winter of 1942-43, had been brutal. A recent thaw in Warsaw, only served to increase the hazards of travel. The main roads were slick with ice. The backroads remained snow covered; commerce and the German military traffic was at a stand-still.

Zygmunt Kaminski leaned against the wall and gathered the ragged cuffs of his threadbare trousers and secured them around his ankles before slipping his feet into the high worker's boots attached to his snowshoes. A worn jacket and a cap with the logo of the Power Company of Warsaw completed the outfit. The snowshoes and the clothes were borrowed, as was the identity card of a utility worker. He was on his way to Old Towne to conduct an interview.

Kaminski's official *Ausbeis*, work permit, from the labor office of the German General Government listed his occupation as Purveyor of Paper Products. His date of birth, 22 September 1906; place of birth, Poznan, a city just outside the German border.

The University of Poznan attracted many German citizens to make their home on the other side of the border, they were known as *Volksdeutsche*. Kaminski's mother, Professor Madeline Bergman was a German citizen. Stefan Kaminski, an engineer, took her German 101 class to boost his communication skills. He took her 102 class to pursue the instructor. Both goals were gratified. In June of 1905 they were wed.

Zygmunt was entitled to the rights of a *Volksdeutscher*; he spoke German like a native. He managed to escape conscription in the *Wehrmacht* in 1938 because of an irregular heartbeat.

The Nazi Blitzkrieg of 1939 rendered his degree in political science useless. Therefore, he turned his talents and skill to the field of journalism and founded an underground newspaper, *Poland's Journal*. This information was not included on his work permit.

≈

General Stefan Rowecki rose from a restless night's sleep. The folding cot was uncomfortable and the thick wool army blanket that doubled as a mattress did little to ease the condition. Rowecki, nom de geurre, "Grot," had slept under worse conditions.

The First World War found him conscripted into the Austro-Hungarian Army. After the war, he spent six months in a cell with a chamber-pot three feet from his bunk for refusing to pledge loyalty to the Austrian Emperor. Upon his release, in 1918, he made his way back to Poland and joined the newly established Polish Army. During the Polish-Soviet War of 1920, he rose to the rank of colonel. Cots and cold ground were familiar to him.

During the invasion of Poland in 1939, Rowecki's unit was crushed. Hitler and Stalin were allies at the start of World War II; they signed a non-aggression pact just days before the attack on Poland. Embedded within a minor clause, they tidily divided the nation of Poland between them. Germany laid claim to land west of the River Bug, and Russia ascribed to the territory east of the river following the ever-elusive Curzon Line.

The onslaught of the combined German and Russian forces that ignited the Second World War battered the Poles into submission. Rowecki fled to Warsaw in October of 1939. The officers and men who survived the battle, gathered whatever arms and munitions they were able to salvage and stored them in the forest where they organized the Home Army, an underground military force.

The leaders and staff of the Polish Government escaped to France, where they continued to operate in exile. Premier Sikorski placed Rowecki in command of the newly established underground militia, the Home Army. With the post came his promotion to general.

He chose 'Grot,' Spearhead, as his nom de guerre. The pseudonym, 'Arrow,' served as his code name for the intelligence division of military operations that he initiated. Pseudonyms were a must, they provided for "no contact upward." The Gestapo's brutal interrogation process could not elicit the true identity of insurgents who were known only by code names.

Military life had been imposed on Rowecki. Eventually, he grew accustomed to the lifestyle. In fact, he considered it a good fit, much the same as the tailored uniform his aide-de-camp, Jetka, had neatly laid on his bunk.

Official headquarters for the underground Home Army was buried securely in the forest, northwest of Warsaw. The annex in Old Towne was surrounded by other buildings that had been reduced to rubble. Four years had gone by, and no one had been assigned the duty of clearing away the aftermath; the area remained isolated in its ruin.

There were no shower facilities. There was no hot water. Grot did the best he could to prepare himself for the day. He kept his thick, dark hair closely cropped, military fashion, but the daily shaving of thick whiskers was chafing his skin. He cringed as he pulled on his uniform; it seemed fresher, and cleaner than he was.

Kitchen appliances were rudimentary. Coffee was boiled in a pot on an electric hot plate; thick dark bread was toasted on a metal device that sat on the burner and heated three slices at a time. Lard with salt and pepper was a convenient spread. A makeshift generator produced the limited power necessary for operating the inadequate quarters.

Jetka sat with him during breakfast to review the agenda for the day. First on the list was an early morning interview with the editor of one of the underground newspapers.

# CHAPTER 2

Kaminski slipped through a lean-to shed that disguised the entrance of the abandoned building. He rapped a code on the basement door. There was a short wait. Perhaps no one heard his knock. He knew the logistics of the building; the office area was a distance from the door. He balled up his fist and was about to knock a second time.

Jetka opened the door and offered a respectful salute. "Good morning Sir, you are expected." He ushered the journalist to the general's desk.

"Pan Zygmunt Kaminski, Sir."

The general quickly covered the file he was working on and placed it in the drawer of his desk. His documents were not for the perusal of a reporter. Early in his military career in the Polish Army, he organized and published the first military weekly periodical. He was familiar with the craft of newsgathering.

He looked up at his visitor and allowed a smile, "Are your tailored suits in the laundry? And where is that familiar *Hamburg*?"

Kaminski ignored the jibe. He removed the worker's cap from his head and pulled up a chair. Rowecki possessed a large ego, and Kaminski had learned how to play on it to get an interesting article. He had been quite successful at drawing a story or two from the commander in the past.

"Is there at least a glass of vodka?"

"Certainly." Grot called out across the expanse of the room, "Jetka, bring two glasses and a bottle."

While the young lieutenant filled their glasses, the general offered a little light banter. His good looks and gift for conversation in social gatherings was disarming. Officers serving under his command rarely caught sight of this side of their commander.

Grot lifted his glass, *"Na zdrovia!"* The two men drained their glasses.

"What's the latest on Chief Delegate Piekalkiewicz?" Kaminski got down to business.

"The Bureau reports that he was arrested and is being held in the S.S Prison on Szucha Street."

"What do you expect will come of this?"

"We'll try to rescue him as soon as possible. No one knows how he will react to the interrogation and torture. He's loaded with information."

"You're concerned that he'll reveal names and places?"

"Of course! We're taking immediate defensive action. Established hideouts will be abolished. Pseudonyms of the important members of the Home Army and Civil Resistance must be changed. It's a nightmare."

"Will you be moving?"

"Not necessarily. This location is not yet known throughout the underground."

Kaminski leaned back in his chair and looked directly into Grot's eyes.

"What can you tell me off the record?"

Grot held the gaze Kaminski thrust on him. "As long as it is definitely 'off the record.'

I'm charting new strategies for Operation Tempest." He made a quick appraisal of his interviewer. Mustn't divulge too much. "I just received a radiogram from Sikorski. He has concerns regarding the original plans."

Sikorski was both premier and commander in chief of the exiled Polish Government. Immediately after the invasion, the administration was transferred to Paris. When the Germans extended their conquering arms to France as well, the premier and his entire staff re-located in London. There would be no quisling government in Poland. The newly established underground government, the Secret State, was headed by a Chief Delegate who took his orders directly from Sikorski. Couriers and covert radio channels maintained an open flow of communication between London and Poland.

Kaminski had been apprised of the plans for an uprising. It was initially proposed during the aftermath of Poland's surrender. The operation was known only to Sikorski and the upper echelon of the underground.

"I thought that was set in stone. Why the change in strategy?"

"The British and the Americans have been threatening to open up a second front, somewhere across the English Chanel, to demolish the Germans. So far, there is nothing to suggest that they are in the process of that mission. Sikorski is concerned that if the allies fail to invade from the west, the Germans will maintain their stronghold, and the plans for Operation Tempest will be doomed."

Kaminski arched an eyebrow. "Is he scrapping the uprising?"

"No. If I read him correctly, he feels the plans for the uprising are too ambitious. With no serious opposition from the west, the Germans will maintain their garrisons here in Poland. In that case, a nationwide uprising would be folly. Control would be minimized, many lives would be lost, and there is every possibility that the Home Army would cease to exist."

"What are your plans? Can you tell me?"

"We need to adopt a manageable uprising. I've worked out a feasible alternative. The rising will occur in three phases."

He rose and made his way to a large map on the wall to emphasize the area he had in mind. "Phase one will begin in the east, in Lwow and Wilno as soon as there is evidence of an invasion by the western allies. Now that the Soviets have ousted the Germans in Stalingrad, Sikorski believes that the Red Army will join our forces, by advancing to the west."

"Plowing us under in their wake."

"My feelings exactly, but Sikorski has taken on the role of diplomat as well as commander in chief."

Kaminski drained his glass and waited for Grot to continue.

"There doesn't seem to be any way of convincing the premier that we are fighting a war with two enemies."

"Is Sikorski's memory failing him? The Russians tore us apart, like a loaf of bread in 1939—half to them and the other half to the Germans. The fact that the Germans turned on them, and invaded their country, doesn't soften Stalin's heart toward Poland."

"So far, my communications with Sikorski have had little effect in jogging his memory or altering his conviction that Russia will rush to our aid to defeat the Germans."

Grot sat back in his chair, visibly agitated by his inability to make his point with Sikorski.

He pulled his posture to attention. "Now that the Soviets have defeated the Germans in Stalingrad, the territory west of the River Bug, held by the Germans, is once more in the possession of the Russians."

He filled his glass with vodka and passed the bottle to Kaminski. Since there was no comment forthcoming, he went on. "Phase two will encompass the zone from the Curzon Line to the Vistula River. Finally, phase three will engage the entire nation. In this manner, we maintain control of the action as we monitor the resistance on our onslaught. This will guarantee full utilization of manpower and weapons, minimizing the cost of lives and ammunition."

"Does this include aid from the Soviets?"

"Sikorski sees Operation Tempest as being beneficial to Stalin as well," Grot spoke matter-of-factly, revealing his concession to the higher authority. "The Red Army is sure to be upon the pre-war borders of Poland before the invasion begins on the second front. With the Allies in their backyard, the Germans are sure to rush to the aid of their Fatherland. Sikorski believes that by combining our forces with the Red Army, the retreating Germans will knuckle under."

"He's delusional. I know the diabolical mind of the Soviets. Believe me, they will leave us in the lurch."

"Kaminski, he's counting on the support of the British. We also have the Americans aiding us with arms and ammunition. However, I can't ignore a gnawing feeling that Stalin is manipulating the Allies to support the Soviet cause, while he undermines ours. The routing of the

Germans out of Stalingrad has made a deep impression on Churchill and Roosevelt. He is flexing his muscles."

"Either they have intentional amnesia, or they are unaware of the tens of thousands—hundreds of thousands, of his own people, that he has murdered. You're right Grot, he will not hesitate to take subversive action against the Poles. Not only does he hate us, but he truly believes Poland is a part of the Soviet Union."

The general sat back in his chair, pondering these remarks. They were valid, but Sikorski was the commander in chief of the Polish Government in London, and the underground Home Army was under his direct orders.

"There are always negative factors. I appreciate your input, Kaminski, as yet, I have been unable to convince Sikorski that Stalin will disappoint us in the end." He gave one last twirl to the glass he held in his hand, downed the vodka and placed it on the desk, concluding the interview.

"I trust your discretion in dispatching only enough information to maintain the security of the operation under the established code. Any copy that you write must first be reviewed by me."

"Whatever I come up with will be for your perusal before I do anything else."

Kaminski sensed the general's utter frustration. The situation was as plane as the nose on your face. Sikorski, formerly a general himself, lauded as a brilliant military strategist, seemed unable to see the destructive consequences that could result from an alliance with Russia. Is this what a diplomatic post does to a man?

It would be better for the Home Army to remain underground until the Russians played out their hand. This was no time for Operation Tempest, no matter what the revisions were. Grot wasn't giving an interview; he was venting his frustration. Kaminski understood the internal conflict the general suffered under Sikorski's mandate. There would be no copy for Grot to review. He would hold the story.

# CHAPTER 3

Some smuggling was better conducted during the night, and Marek Gudzynski, aka Dysthmus, had gone through the week with promises of catching up on his sleep. It was near the curfew hour, after a particularly vexing day of covert deliveries, and he was on his way home to fulfill his promise, after a quick drink.

His boyhood friend, Kazek, operated a family-owned bar and restaurant that was frequented by working class residents in the center of Warsaw. The bar itself, was over three-hundred years old. Booths sat along the window wall and small tables dotted the floor to hold chess and checker boards for patrons to while away the hours while they ate salty pretzels and drank pitchers of beer.

An old sot, who went about town begging for the price of a drink, was the only one left in the place. Kazek was trying to rouse the old man so that he could lock up, when Dysthmus walked in.

"I won't stay long, Kazek. I need to get some sleep. I just need a drink and a word with a friend."

"Don't push your luck. I'm not feeling very friendly tonight, and I want to get out of here." He pulled a bottle of vodka off the shelf and poured his pushy customer a drink.

Dysthmus sipped his vodka. The mirror in front of him reflected a firm chin, high cheek bones and plain brown eyes that caught the sparkle of the rogue within whenever he smiled. His face was set off by a widow's peak of thick, dark hair. "I have to get a work certificate," he mused as he stared at his image. "The doctors in town will no longer write prescriptions for me. They say I've had every ailment known to man and they refuse to take the risk of being discovered by the police and charged with malpractice." He drained his glass and pushed it forward for a refill.

Kazek smiled wryly and obliged his friend with another drink.

"Do you know where I can get a job?"

The old sot lifted his head, "Try the Labor office. They need slaves to labor for them in Germany."

Kazek was surprised that the old man was awake and coherent. "Okay, Jozef, you've had enough." He lifted him from his seat and struggled to get the drunk's flaccid body out the door.

"I don't know why I let that drunk in here."

"Because you feel sorry for him. He probably spent his pay check in here before the war. You owe him something."

"Go to hell!"

Kazek stood at the door, a signal that he was waiting to lock up, when Ryk, from the secret radio station pushed in on them.

"Dysthmus, I thought I'd find you here." His tone was not pleasant. "I stopped by your room and spoke to your neighbors; no one knew where you were."

"They never do!"

Dysthmus, grabbed the bottle of vodka from the bar and reached over the bar for a glass, "Ryk, my buddy, have a drink."

"No, thank you. I have to get back to Praga before curfew. I could get caught. I'm on duty for the night." He looked intently at Dysthmus, as if to gauge his level of sobriety. "The BBC just signed off with the signal tune. The others are already on their way to the site. I have to get back." He turned to leave, "You better get a move on." He flung the warning over his shoulder.

The message had just arrived via short wave radio from London. All of the conditions and stipulations for an Allied arms drop had been arranged weeks before. If, and when the weather was conducive to a relatively safe flight, a team of five insurgents were scheduled to meet at a pre-arranged site to collect the booty. The recording of a popular wartime song at the conclusion of the nightly BBC broadcast would be their signal for, "all systems go."

Dysthmus grabbed his coat and cap, gulped down the rest of his drink and headed out the door. He hopped into his truck and took off without turning on the headlights. He would depend on his adequate night vision, his intrinsic knowledge of the roads, and his guardian angel to get him out of the watchful eye of the gendarmes in Center City.

The strafing of the airport by the Luftwaffe, during the invasion of 1939, inflicted major potholes on the runways. The Germans saw no need to restore the landing field for future use and the potholes remained. A sharp eye in daylight might determine the remnant of the main landing strip. At night, the terrain appeared to be a vacant dumpsite. Scattered about were broken bits of the lanterns that once guided the planes into a smooth and balanced landing. The field became home to groundhogs and other vermin.

The proposed "drop" of weapons and ammunition by the RAF was due at approximately two a.m. "Approximately," conveyed the possibility of the deviation of an hour or two, either way. Dysthmus looked about to establish the positions of two other trucks already lying-in wait under the full moon.

The loneliness of the place released the demons of past memories that he fought to ignore. Five children in a small flat. His father did odd jobs for the undertaker, his mother took the children with her on trash days as they wove their way in and out of streets where the wealthy lived. He was seven years old when he rescued a wagon from the trash. He converted it to a shopping cart, which was used to haul the bread and milk that he stole from the doorsteps of these very same streets. Breakfast was the one meal the family could be sure of.

He tried to fall asleep, but he was too unsettled. He rationalized that a slug of vodka might act as a stimulant, change his focus, and add some comfort to an unpleasant situation. There was more than half a bottle left. He periodically measured off a few drams at a time, as if he were following a prescription. Relief came slowly as he drifted into a deep sleep.

The noisy drone of a low flying plane woke him. A surge of adrenaline sparked him into action. He hopped out of the truck, yanked a book of matches from his pocket and struck one against the heel of his shoe. The light would serve to announce his position to the pilot and the other four retrievers.

The belly of the plane opened, and the billowing parachutes drifted gracefully to the ground to deposit the heavy artillery and ammunition. The rhythmic thump, thump, of the objects as they hit the ground soon became the only sound to be heard, as the plane continued on its flight.

This recent cache included several British Sten guns, grenades, ammunition, and a load of pistols. Dysthmus wrapped the 'gifts' he retrieved within the parachutes that buoyed them. The women of Civil Resistance would find many uses for the luxurious silk fabric.

The other two trucks took off, leaving two guns and a large packet of unknown contents behind for Dysthmus to collect. He started toward the large packet, there might be American dollars inside. The sound of approaching vehicles ignited the panic button in his belly. He flung the package into the truck, shoved the tailgate in place, and ran around to the cab. Once inside, he jammed the accelerator to the floor and muttered a fervent prayer as he fled the scene.

He caught the flashing lights of two autos in the reflection of his rear-view mirror. Gendarmes, no doubt about it. They were descending on him at top speed. His old truck would never out race them. He had driven this road many times and knew every bump and turn. At a sharp curve, Dysthmus jerked the wheel sharply to the right and rammed the accelerator to the floor. The truck careened off the shoulder of the road and bounced along the strip of underbrush until it burrowed into a hammock of trees. He cut off the engine and listened for the sound of the roaring motors as they sped on down the road.

The adrenaline had served its purpose, but now that he had managed to escape the arm of the law, he was completely enervated.

He reached under the seat for the bottle of vodka, drained the contents, lit a cigarette, and offered a prayer to the Blessed Virgin—in thanksgiving.

# CHAPTER 4

A warm breeze ruffled the curtains in the little kitchen window. There was an early thaw; the birches and oaks were teased into exposing patches of green. Father Jan Lipinski sat eating his breakfast; he didn't like the fuss of the formal dining room. On Tuesdays, there was only one mass for the day, and the priest was able to have his breakfast earlier than usual. He stretched his long legs under the small table and spread out the latest edition of the *Nowy Kourier Warszawski*. The newspaper was printed in the Polish language by the Germans for propaganda purposes, and to keep the Poles informed of current edicts and restrictions. The Germans had restricted the lives of the citizens of Warsaw in every possible way. If anything, life had become more difficult in 1943 than it was at the onset of the occupation. Yet, daily mass went on as usual, with a surprising number of Germans showing up for confession and communion.

There was a re-print of the article of the capture of Professor Jan Piekalkiewicz, the chief delegate of civil resistance. The Gestapo were reveling at their arrest of the leader of the Secret State. The professor had boarded a tram and was on his way to conduct a secret meeting with one of the many organizations of the underground. He never arrived at his destination.

The priest read between the lines of propaganda and turned to the page with the heading, "RECENT ATROCITIES." These were not the heinous acts of the occupying forces, but the recent accounts of sabotage and retribution, which the underground imposed on the Nazis.

First on the list of offenses was the notice:

Atrocity in Grojek: Olaf Ehrlick, manager of farm quotas, was murdered by unknown assailants. Penalty was enforced on thirty-four civilians who were shot in retribution.

He was interrupted by a soft knock on the swinging door that connected to the dining room. Father Pawil, rector of St. Basil, a church just outside of Warsaw, entered with a slight bow of his head and a meager spread to his lips.

"Good morning, Jan; I see you have the news at hand."

"Good morning Henryk. Yes, thirty-four peasants murdered in reprisal for the death of one German."

Pawel nodded his head, "The Peasant Battalion had received an order from the Secret Court for his assassination. He was accused of setting fire to fields of farmers, who had not met their quota. As a barbarous act of reprisal, and to set an example to the other farmers in the area, the Wyzek family was burned alive in their barn."

Father Lipinski shuddered and bowed his head in silent prayer for the deceased and tortured. Father Pawil joined him.

Lipinski raised his head. "Where's the rational for that sort of action? It only makes it more difficult for the farmers to get the quota together, not to mention the waste." He looked out the window and allowed his gaze to rest on the sprouting buds on the trees. Spring, the regeneration of life.

"Forgive me, Henryk, I forgot my manners. Have you had your breakfast yet?"

"This is a day of fasting for me."

Father Jan looked at his friend's hollow cheeks and feverishly shining eyes; he breathed a long sigh. It did no good to caution Father Pawil about the harmful outcome of sustained fasting. He was a mystic, who fed off the Holy Spirit within him.

"May I pour you some coffee?"

"Yes, please." He adjusted his cassock and sat in the seat opposite his friend and associate."

Father Jan rinsed a cup that had been sitting on the drain and filled it with coffee. He apprised Father Pawil of the latest bit of news he had gleaned from the clergy grapevine.

"The Cardinal once again has refused an invitation to meet with Governor Frank. I must admit, I have my concerns regarding His Eminence's thwarting the advances made by the Governor."

Father Pawil poured some of his coffee into his saucer and sipped on the hot brew. "His Eminence has total trust in God; whatever the reprisals might be."

"Yes, but that is not Frank's way of operating. He has a short fuse and a long memory. There are bound to be repercussions."

"Perhaps the Governor's faith delays any reprisals. He is Catholic."

"That's like saying the devil was baptized." He lifted his cup to his lips and looked over the rim into Pawil's eyes. "You may be right, Father, I hope so."

There was a pause in the conversation while the two men reflected on possible repercussions that might be foisted upon the cardinal, whose residence was just a short distance from the Governor General's headquarters within Wawel Castle in Cracow.

Pawel resumed the conversation, "The struggle against the Germans stiffens. The quotas on farm products leaves very little for the farmers to subsist on, the entire population within the General Government is on starvation rations. The transportation of contraband items becomes more difficult. Just the other night, Dysthmus, the main delivery man for the Home Army, was almost captured with a shipment of munitions he picked up from a recent parachute drop. The Angel of the Lord had to be with him."

Father Jan straightened his posture. "Was he able to deliver the munitions to the commander?"

"Yes, but he is lying low. The Home Army and Civil Resistance count on his deliveries. I don't know what they will do in the meantime."

Father Jan's church was centered in Warsaw and vital information from the underground was coded and issued from his pulpit to assist in the disturbance of the General Government. Other parish priests used the same procedure for any underground activity that was specific to their immediate region. A relay operation was used to spread through the network. Each church was responsible for delivering the dispatch to its neighboring parish.

Father Jan reached for his bible and began to shuffle through the pages; his finger paused in the New Testament. "We need to alert the parishes about this recent development. There are those who will be looking for their regular deliveries." He reached for pad and pencil. "In the homily this Sunday, we will deliver the message from Romans 8:25 *"But if we hope for what we do not see, we eagerly wait for it with perseverance"*. He made a note of the passage and then handed it to Father Pawil. "Spread the message, and have the priests present it within the agreed upon cue."

"I shall start the relay mission as soon as I get back to my parish."

"Yes, and have the priests use the phrase, 'Father deliver us our daily bread,' before the cue, so as to reinforce the meaning."

Dysthmus maneuvered his freight truck into the narrow alley of an industrial site in Old Town. The freshly painted markings on the truck labeled it as one belonging to Schultz Sewing Machine, an old established German firm in Poland that was currently producing munitions for the Germans. He parked the truck on the grass of the unkempt garden. Although the weather was warming, the ground still carried the frost from a particularly hard winter; he would have no trouble gaining traction once he completed his mission.

He entered a foundry and went into the basement. From there, he made his way through a tunnel into the adjacent building where the Home Army's underground newspaper, under the auspices of the Bureau Intelligence, made its home. The resounding clamor from the foundry drowned the sound of the printing press.

He used a hammer to tap his special code on the concealed door of the foundation wall, two very loud knocks, followed by a ten second pause, and then three short knocks. The door pushed open; a short stocky man poked his head out and smiled up at him.

"Dysthmus, I hear you're out of business. What can I do for you?"

"Plenty!" He slid inside the door and slammed it shut. "Listen Levik, I've managed to get hold of some documents of the General Government. The official passes are marked 'Urgent,' to get deliveries of vital German materials past the gendarme without a search." He handed his packet to Levik. "Would you duplicate this for me?"

"Come in, come in." He said as he shoved the wheeled pallet, stacked with bales of paper, back to its original place to cover the illicit door.

"Follow me."

Levik led Dysthmus to his desk and climbed up on his stool to carefully examine the documents within the packet. With a black pen, he drew a broad band, diagonally, across a blank piece of paper.

"We'll make this that ugly olive green that the Nazis use for their military." He then printed bold black capital letters across the band, URGENT. "How's that?"

"Perfect! That'll get me moving along without being discovered."

"Now wait a minute, Dysthmus." He hopped off his stool and walked over to the wall behind his desk. He removed a cinder block and pulled out an object.

"This is the official stamp of the Governor General's signature. Everything you need will be fastidiously duplicated."

Dysthmus grinned, "Wonderful! But I'll need a way to inform the gendarme of the new process, or else they might call for confirmation."

"We'll make circulars with the facsimile of the new pass. For this you must give me time. I must give them an authentic appearance, as they will be mailed from the Governor General's office."

He led Dysthmus to the door. "Come by this Friday, I'll show you what we have for you."

# CHAPTER 5

Three black autos were parked around building number 16 on Zielona Street. They wore the markings of the dreaded swastika.

Michal Bednarek walked up the street to his apartment, which was directly across the street from the disturbance. He felt the need to establish himself as an employed citizen; he shifted the handle of his briefcase to his left hand, making it more visible to onlookers across the street. The sight of the swastikas triggered the hairs on the back of his neck to rise. He kept his gaze straight in front of him and made an effort to appear nonchalant as he slipped into the front door of his building.

His steps were brisk as he walked through the hall. A man in his fifties, Michal cut a youthful figure. His blonde hair and fair coloring made him appear years younger than his professional background might imply. His carriage and demeanor, his very wardrobe, signaled conservatism. He reached into his pocket for his keys. Before he withdrew them, the door was opened by Janina, the maid.

"Pan, they have come for Tavish!"

"Yes, I see." He shut the door behind him and went to the front window where he could observe the street, being careful not to touch the lace curtains and find himself being observed.

"How long have they been there?"

"Maybe ten minutes before you arrived." She stood behind him, not taking her eyes off the drama that was unfolding in front of the old man's apartment.

They watched as the front door of the building opened and two Gestapo agents led the way down the steps. They were followed by two more agents who flanked either side of the old man, as they jostled him down the stairs. Tavish appeared quite disheveled; blood was streaming from his forehead. Another pair of agents took up the rear carrying large cardboard boxes.

A shiver ran through him as he watched the old man being shoved into the car, as if he were some useless bag of freight that had to be transported swiftly away. Janina covered her eyes with her apron and was sobbing uncontrollably.

He turned around and gently put his arm around her. "There, there, Janina, he knew this day would come. He was a relentless old tiger bent on fighting the system."

He pulled away from her and lifted her face to look in her eyes. "Janina, I must go to the Gestapo Headquarters to investigate the situation."

He allowed her a moment to gain some control. "Listen, you must not say anything of this to Pani Leona and Irena. I don't want to have them unduly upset. I will apprise them of the situation when I get home. Don't wait dinner for me."

"What shall I say?"

"Tell them I have gone back to the office to meet with a client, and I will be home directly. If they ask you about Tavish, tell them only what you saw, and don't mention the shape he was in. And for God's sake, don't tell them that I've gone to Szucha Street."

Janina had somehow managed to prepare an agreeable enough meal, under the circumstances. Unsure of her ability to answer the women's questions, she rehearsed her response within the framework Pan Bednarek had allowed her. The sound of the women's approaching voices filled the hall and Janina offered a Hail Mary. She wiped her hands on her apron, straightened her hair and went to the door, still rehearsing the lines she would deliver.

Pani Leona spoke first. "Janina, what has happened? The neighbors were upon us with reports of the Gestapo taking Tavish away."

"They did Pani, around five-thirty."

Irena removed her jacket and handed it to the maid. "Did you see what happened, Janina?"

"Yes, from the front window. I watched from the time I saw the Gestapo cars come up the street, until they took him away."

Leona made no attempt to take off the jacket she wore. Slender and petite, she seemed to shrink within it as she clutched it close to her. She stood by the door shaking her head. She had known the old politician all her life. She made no effort to stifle her tears.

Irena glanced around the foyer for signs of her father's presence. "Has Tata come home?"

"He is at the office, working on a new account. He said not to wait dinner." She replied in the rehearsed manner she had prepared.

Leona grabbed her daughter's hand. "He's gone to Szucha Street to find out what they have on Tavish."

Bednarek warily approached the building on Szucha Street. The former home of the Ministry of Education, it now housed the administrative offices of the SS. Two armed guards stood sentry at the front door and required that he present his identification card. One of the officers demanded, "What is your purpose?"

He handed him a business card. The card that announced his former profession.

Michal J. Bednarek, Attorney at Law

"I'm here to represent a client of mine, and I need to see Commandant Stroop."

The guard snapped the identification card back to him. "Follow me."

Bednarek fell in step to walk the hall he was so familiar with. The guard stopped abruptly in front of one of the offices on the right. The frosted glass portion of the door had the printed inscription, SS-Brigadefuhrer Jurgen Stroop. The guard presented three sharp knocks on the door and waited for a response. Presently, a uniformed soldier appeared wearing the rank of sergeant on his sleeve.

"This is Attorney Bednarek, here to see the commandant." The guard deposited the visitor and took off.

"Good evening, Pan. What gives you to think that the commander is here at this late hour?"

"Good evening, Officer, perhaps a hunch that the commander might be here to arrange the internment of a client of mine, who has just been arrested."

"Ah, Pan Tavish holds your interest. Have a seat; I'll announce you."

Tavish was well into his seventies. Widowed, he lived alone in the apartment which had at one time housed his wife and family. Through all the years of his active participation in politics, this was not only his home, but his office where he conducted his business. He continued his practice of seeing old friends and new. That was an intricate part of his life style. For a while, the Germans paid no attention to the old man. However, he was deeply embroiled in conspiracy, living for the day Poland would be independent. With all the visitors who came and went, doubtless someone informed on him.

Either Stroop was involved with matters on his desk, or he had gone to his dinner. Bednarek warmed the seat for an hour and half. It was after eight when the sergeant reappeared.

"Commandant Stroop will see you now."

The Brigadefuhrer greeted him by standing up from his desk. He extended his hand. "Good evening, Pan Bednarek. Sorry to have kept you waiting. How may I be of service?"

Bednarek was in no condition to mince words. "I'm here to see Ignatz Tavish."

Stroop drew himself into full military posture. "There will be no legal representation for him."

Bednarek's face reddened under this provocative statement. He blustered and was about to respond that he was here as a courtesy to a client.

"This is not a civil case, Pan Bednarek. Your client is guilty of conspiracy against the General Government."

Bednarek knew the game rules, but he felt compelled to make an appearance, if only to satisfy his concern for the old man's predicament. He was not about to lend dignity to Stroop's comment by responding. The prescribed Nazi procedure for conspiracy was irrevocable. He tipped his hat and was about to leave.

"Let me caution you, Bednarek. You do not want to go about defending people inciting against the German authority. You stand the risk of being considered a conspirator as well."

Bednarek bristled to attention. "Commandant Stroop, my family has been engaged in professional service of one kind or another for over two hundred years. We do not yield to political circumstances that disrupt our community. That is a fruitless venture; politics are forever changing. We focus on performing our professional duties. I practice the law, not conspiracy."

Stroop took his seat and sneered up at Michal.

"So, you continue to practice law? Where are you getting your clients? Can any Pole afford to pay legal fees at this time?"

Bednarek's emotional fervor gave way to self-effacement. In reality, his clients had dwindled away. The Germans had confiscated all business ventures in Poland, and the only cases Michal now handled were civil cases between Poles. Any cases involving Germans were tried in the German court. He was earning his living as an accountant, a position he held as a student while he worked his way through law school. His clients were the wealthy Schindlerites, entrepreneurs from Germany, who bought the confiscated businesses of Poles at a severely reduced price.

"I still have a legal client or two."

"Then concentrate on them, if you value your neck, and leave the conspirators alone; or you may be considered in league with the partisans."

He called out to the Sargent, "Show this prominent lawyer the way out." He smirked, "The next time he appears in this office, there may not be a way out."

# CHAPTER 6

Dysthmus smiled, his visit would coincide with the Duzat's Sunday breakfast, and he was bringing a good appetite to appreciate Ludwiga's cooking. His tangible gifts were three pounds of coffee and two pounds of sugar.

During the reconditioning of his truck, he had been allocated a respectable German car, a dark green Opel Kapitan, along with forged documents and a forged driver's license. He was sure his new vehicle would make an impression on the Duzats.

There was no one outside the house; a good sign that they were in the kitchen, enjoying *kielbasa* and eggs. He parked the car in the drive, picked up his gift packages and sauntered up the walk.

Fredryk Duzat opened the screen door.

"Marek, I heard the car and wondered if it was the Gestapo in that ugly Nazi automobile."

He held the door open for the package bearing guest. "So, you're still alive and well. The devil doesn't want you."

Marek smiled broadly. Fredryk was his favorite of the Duzat boys. He had a common sense, easy approach to life; unlike his older brother, Vitzek, who concentrated on the yield of production on the farm, and rarely laughed.

"No, I hear he's looking for you." He juggled his packages into the crook of his left arm allowing him a free hand to wrap around his friend while he placed a kiss on his cheek.

"Come in, you hapless beggar." He turned his head in the direction of the kitchen to call his daughter, "Pola, that ugly guy Marek is here to see you. Shall I let him in?"

A shriek was heard from the kitchen as Pola rushed to the porch.

"*Kochanek*, Love!" was her only verbal greeting. She threw her arms around him.

The relationship between them was strictly one sided. Marek enjoyed the company of a variety of women within his wide distribution area. He saw Pola as the delightful daughter of Fredryk Duzat. She was seventeen, too young to consider in any other way. Pola, however, had an intense crush on this dark and exciting man of mystery.

Marek looked at Fredryk and shrugged his shoulders. With the packages in his arms, there was no way for him to give an appropriate response. Fredryk grinned and relieved him of the coffee and sugar. He went inside and allowed the couple a few moments to themselves. Pola would never forgive him if he didn't.

Vapors of past meals of stuffed cabbage and beet soup hovered in the air while *kielbasa* and bacon added yet another layer to mingle in the mist after Sunday breakfast. The family was seated at the large linden wood table, relaxing over the last sips of coffee and *panchki*, Polish style donuts.

Vitzek's wife, Halina, fired questions at Marek as soon as he entered the kitchen. "Father Pawil alerted us of the possibility of a delay in future deliveries in his coded sermon this morning."

Vitzek added, "I spoke with him, confidentially, after mass and he said you were almost caught by the gendarmes."

The elderly Ludwiga was years beyond feeling the excitement of adventure and intrigue. Life to her was black and white, day and night. She brought an extra plate to the table and abruptly interrupted the inquiries, "Thank you for the coffee, Marek. We are all out. Eat! I'll make a fresh pot."

"There is no reason for thanks. It's small payment for my breakfast."

He picked up his fork and started to eat while he gave an account of his recent encounter with the gendarmes. "I still had a few items to pick up, after the two other trucks took off, when I heard the sound of motors behind me. I never got around to retrieving them. I tossed the package I had just picked up into the truck, slammed the tailgate shut, and ran for the cab to start the motor. I guess I knew those back roads better than my pursuers, but I'm sure they got a description of the truck."

Ludwiga admonished him. "Eat! They can wait for the story; your food grows cold."

Marek followed orders. "Ludwiga, my favorite cook, how are things going with the family food distribution?" He reached for a *panchki* and Ludwiga refilled his cup with coffee.

"Well, enough, Marek. Although I must say, we women are better distributors than you."

"How so, Matka?"

"We don't get caught!"

Vitzek's son, Felix laughed. "That's true! Bapca, Mamma, and Aunt Matcha are known as the big-busted women of Sochaczew. The contraband food sewn into their clothing is winning the admiration of all the passengers on the train as they ride into Warsaw. The men are impressed with the breadth of their breasts." He burst into laughter.

Fredryk and Dysthmus bit their lips and lowered their heads.

Felix tried to compose himself. "The last time they came through the market to drop off their provisions to Civil Resistance, Aunt Matcha's fat shifted when she walked, and that got her more admiring glances." He lost control and gave vent to the humorous image he had evoked.

"Bravo! Matka, but you weren't listening. I was found out—not caught." Marek pinched her cheek and went on with his story.

"I don't know how many times our unit made these pickups in the past. The whole operation was second nature to me. I can't help feeling that someone informed on us."

Fredryk rose from the table. "Bring your cup; we are going out on the porch for a smoke while the clever women clean the kitchen."

The men lit up their tobacco of choice. Vitzek and Fredryk puffed up a glowing blaze in their pipe bowls. Felix offered to roll a cigarette for Dysthmus.

"No, thank you," he waved it off, "Here, have a Swan,"—the pre-war top selling brand.

"So, what's with the ugly green auto?" Fredryk challenged him.

"I have obtained a working certificate and while my truck was in the garage for overhauling and a new paint job, Grot issued the Opel." He raised his head and blew a smoke ring in the air. "I am now gainfully employed by the Schultz Sewing Machine Company, and that name has been skillfully inscribed on the panels of my truck. The Home Army print shop has provided me with new identity cards."

He pulled the cards from the pocket of his leather jacket and handed them to Fredryk. Vitzek leaned over to examine them. The cards identified the bearer as Viktor Dielinski, Truck Driver.

"The Opel Kapitan is a bonus, thrown in. It's mine to use for scouting and reconnaissance missions."

"How did you manage to get the position?"

"A loyal partisan is the dispatcher for shipment of weapons and ammunition that Schultz is manufacturing now." He smiled, "I'm all set up, nice and proper."

"Marek, what plans do you have to resume operations?"

The farmers of the underground Peasant Battalion, shaved off as much of their crops as possible for civil resistance to distribute to the starving citizens. Marek was in charge of the transportation of the contraband produce.

"That I have plans is one thing. That I can accomplish them is another. I am waiting on the delivery of some official looking documents that will get my truck through the gendarmes without an inspection. Something like what the Government General uses."

"Civil Resistance will benefit from that!" Felix blurted.

Vitzek delivered a stern look his way. He was deeply troubled by his son's involvement with the underground. Twenty-two years may qualify him as an adult, but wisdom doesn't always come along with the rights and privileges of a young man.

"Come with me, Marek, I have something to show you." He led the way to the barn.

He maneuvered his way behind a tractor and pulled out a box from a recess in the wall. He opened the lid as he approached Marek.

"Here, this is the latest instruction from the Directorate of Civil Resistance, regarding quotas of farm products."

He handed him the printed document, "We are about to take a stand against the outrageous quota demands of the Germans."

Marek read the instructions which advocated a disruption to the railways and the shipment of farm quotas. "There are no specifics."

"I'm waiting to hear from commander Furtak."

"Be careful! You know how your parents feel about your involvement in the insurrection."

# CHAPTER 7

Felix Duzat operated the family stall in the Open Market of Warsaw. He had his usual customers, many of them were also members of the civil resistance. His stall was one of several sites within the city that was considered secure enough for partisans to swap underground information. On Monday of that week, he obtained the coded instructions for Operation Rail. He copied the message and placed the folded copy in his package of cigarettes.

On Wednesday, Felix drove a wagon load of produce into Warsaw. He unloaded his baskets and set them up on the shelves of his stall. At ten o'clock, he placed a 'CLOSED' sign on the top shelf and asked the peddler in the next stall to keep an eye on things while he went to the toilet.

The café at the end of the square had a few tables set out on the street during the unseasonably warm weather. This provided a certain ambiance, but it was not conducive to conversation; the noise from the Open Market offered too much competition.

Dysthmus arrived at the café, ordered a cup of coffee, and took it outside. The tables were empty; there was always a lull between breakfast and lunch. He took a seat at a table near the street and spread a newspaper before him. He was on the lookout for Felix.

He watched as Felix went directly inside the café. A few minutes later, he emerged from the doorway and feigned surprise at seeing Dysthmus sitting at the table. He waved as he approached him. "How's the coffee?"

"Flavored hot water, not coffee." He pushed the other chair away from the table with his foot. "Join me."

"Flavored hot water is not for me, but I'll have a smoke with you."

Dysthmus was impressed. "Swan cigarettes? That's an expensive brand." He thumped the package in his palm and slid a slender cylinder from the small slit at the top. "Where's your very own roll-em cigarettes?"

"I made a delivery to the mayor's office and found these lying on his desk."

After a brief exchange of small talk, Felix rose from the table and loudly reported that he had to get back to the market to relieve his friend who was watching his stall. He left the empty cigarette pack on the table. Under his breath, he murmured, "Furtak has need of you."

Dysthmus picked up the cigarette pack, along with his change and his keys, and walked back to his car.

The Socialist Armed Organization was communist in its origin and focused on railway sabotage as its practice. Veterans of rail service discipline and the regulation of time schedules, they were every bit as meticulous as the Germans in keeping records.

The rails were the arteries that carried military supplies to the Nazi garrisons and transported the produce and livestock out of Poland to Berlin. They were of vital importance to the German war effort.

Initially, the SOA used ordinary railway mines that exploded under the first train and caused a disruption of four hours. They upgraded their skill by adding chemical substances to the grease-bins to stall the engines. Hand crafted bombs were buried into the coalbins to ignite the furnaces. In 1940, the disruption of rail service caused breakdowns that disabled engines for fourteen hours.

The ordinary single railway mine was improved upon. A chain of mines set along the tracks automatically exploded in a sequenced pattern. The first exploded when the train went over it. Two more, placed on either side, blew up when rescue trains approached from either side of the wrecked supply train. Total loss to the German Government: one supply train and two repair trains, plus ten miles of track.

By 1943, the added ingredients to the grease-bins and coalbins increased the estimated time for repairs to an engine up to fourteen days. At one point, railroad maintenance shops, all over Poland reported two-hundred engines withdrawn from service for repairs. Time spent on the restoration of an engine depended on how quickly the engineer realized he had a problem and sent the engine to the repair shop. Withdrawal from service could last from three days to three months. At one point, rail traffic in Poland was completely disrupted for three weeks.

The foreman of the Sochaczew-Warsaw line, Bolchek, a staunch member of the party, had been instructed by his superior to conduct a disruption aboard the freight cars that were carrying top grade grain bound for Berlin. Bolchek contacted the local Peasant Battalion to request additional manpower. The commander of the unit, Furtak, met with him at the station.

Bolchek's corpulent body filled his desk chair, and then some. A large plug of tobacco bulged in his left cheek.

"On Wednesday, of next week, freight wagons will be loaded with quotas of prime grain for shipment to Germany." He skillfully controlled the tobacco juice while he spoke.

"How many wagons?"

"Three. And we know exactly where they will be placed on the line, so it will be easy to accomplish the disruption within the allotted time."

"Just what kind of disruption?"

Bolchek ushered the commander outside to set the scene. "We'll split the sacks open and spill the grain out on the tracks." Bolchek spit the juice of his tobacco onto the tracks, as though to emphasize the spot he had in mind. "Poles are starving, and the best of our grain goes to the Nazis."

The standard monthly rations for civilians was down to five-hundred-sixty-three calories a day. There had been a steady decline from January of 1941, when the daily caloric intake was eight-hundred-sixty-three calories a day. Furtak, himself a farmer, could not justify the waste of grain that would result from this action. Thumbing the nose at the Germans held little credence in the face of mounting starvation.

"Three carloads of grain are a considerable amount. At best, only a trifling of it could be salvaged by the local peasants"

"And I'm sure they'll be grateful for it." Bolchek crowed.

"Why waste all that grain? Surely we could salvage it for the hungry."

Bolchek snapped back, "I have a schedule to keep."

He left Furtak outside and went back to his desk, shutting the door behind him. The commander walked away, unsettled.

During the meeting of the troops, Furtak went over the logistics and timing involved in the disruption. "Bolchek insists that we spill the grain on the ground."

Grumbling among the men gave Furtak a cue that they were on the same page.

"He says timing is crucial to the success of the disruption. There is no time to salvage the grain."

Piotreck, rubbed the thick, gray beard on his chin. "It's already in sacks; isn't it?"

"Yes. But how will we unload the grain?"

Felix spoke up. "Dysthmus. He already knows we are going to be involved in the disruption of farm quotas. We'll load it onto his truck; he'll deliver it to Civil Resistance."

"Good!" There was a faint look of triumph in Furtak's smile.

"You contact him and bring him on board."

Dysthmus pulled up in his truck at the appointed hour in the middle of a heated exchange between Bolchek and Furtak. He pursed his lips and pushed his cap back on his head. The discussion ended with Bolchek turning his back on Furtak and waving the peasants on to begin the unloading. Furtak threw his hat on the ground and hurled an expletive Bolchek's way.

Dysthmus hopped out of his truck and ran up to the foreman. "Bolchek, I have my truck here. We could unload your cargo and I'll deliver it to Civil Resistance to distribute to the citizens of Warsaw."

"Well, that's good for the citizens, but I am limited to the time I have to destroy the freight before the Nazis come around."

Furtak intervened, "My men are fast workers. Give us a try. If we're running short on your schedule, we'll quit and do what it was you set out to do. But at least let us try to salvage some of this."

Once he agreed to go ahead with the plan, Bolchek took charge of the loading process to maintain control over his time constraints. Dysthmus' truck was quickly filled, and the left-over sacks were slashed; the grain poured onto the ground. The nearby residents would benefit from the debris.

Then, Bolchek made an unexpected move. He ordered his men to pour petrol into the cars and take a torch to them. The flames from the ignited petrol sent a fiery orange glow billowing to the sky. In a few minutes, sirens could be heard screaming in the night. An alarm had been set. The Peasant Battalion quickly dispersed. Dysthmus thrust the truck into gear and stormed down the road.

# CHAPTER 8

A heavy mood hung over the breakfast table. Michal Bednarek found the item referring to Tavish in the *Nowy Kourier*.

Ignatz Tavish, former official of Polish Parliament, was arrested and charged with insurrection against the General Government. His documents were seized, and names of other insurgents are now in the hands of S. S. Brigadefuhrer Stroop. Further action is at hand.

Michael handed the paper to Leona. "They're entertaining another fright campaign. Everyone who knew Tavish is squirming in their seats."

She read the article and then reached for the coffee pot for a refill.

"Have you nothing to say?"

"What is there to say? I am squirming in my seat. Are you not doing so also?"

"No, Leona, I am not! I do my job and do not involve myself in underground activities. But you have every reason to squirm."

She took a deep breath; she knew what was coming.

"What will you do about your scheduled meetings? There is no way that you can continue them under this roof. This is currently a crime zone. Gendarme and the Blue Police are all over the place." He waited for a reply.

Leona sipped her coffee and turned the page of the newspaper in front of her.

Michal thrust his napkin on the table. "Leona, answer me!"

"Michal what can I say? I have to make other arrangements; frankly right now, I just can't know what to do."

"Then let me tell you what you must do. Your teaching days are over for the duration of the war."

She leaned back in her chair and stared out the window that lent full view to the building where Tavish had been arrested.

Hitler had closed the universities and secondary schools in October of 1940, leaving only the elementary schools, grades one to four, to provide rudimentary lessons that would ensure a population of lower-level workers to perform in the German labor market. Governor Frank appraised the situation, *"The Poles are to supply only labor and it will suffice if they can simply read and write..."*

Professor of history, Leona Bednarek lost her position and the university that had employed her for sixteen years. The university was closed, and the professors went into hiding to escape being executed as members of the elite. She quickly arranged to conduct clandestine meetings in her home to a group of dedicated students who were working toward their degrees.

There was an entire network of underground university studies. Professors risked their lives to teach their subjects in established hide outs located throughout the city and its suburbs. Forged certificates and diplomas were dated 1938 and 1939, to present authenticity to the documents. As a result, several hundred students received their degrees during the German occupation.

Michal left his place at the table and walked around to his wife's chair. He took her chin in his hand and lifted her face to look in her eyes.

He whispered, "Think this over, my dear. I know how much the university and the students mean to you, but it's not worth a death warrant."

Leona remained at the table after Michal left for the day. She aimlessly turned the pages of the newspaper, with only a slight awareness of what she was reading, until she came across another fright article.

Vandals in Sochaczew have destroyed the contents of three freight cars filled with grain bound for Germany, and then set fire to the cars.

Eighteen people from the village were shot in retribution. Gestapo agents are investigating the situation and very soon the responsible parties will be brought to justice.

Saturday morning, Leona Bednarek chose her light weight gray suit. She removed the curlers from her hair and ran a brush through the thick dark tresses that were a tinge too long for a mature woman. It was ages since she had a perm; she would have to find the time to get a haircut. Meanwhile, the dimples in her cheek and the bright green of her eyes made up for any lack of cosmetics she was forced to do without.

She left the apartment without breakfast or coffee; she was on her way to church. Confession was offered after mass on Saturday. Leona had been to confession within the month, so there was no urgency on her part to seek reconciliation. She had need of a private consult with Father Lipinski; the confessional offered just such a convenience.

The Church was in the throes of Lent and there were more penitents than usual. Leona hated queues; she wasn't much good at idle waiting. The door of the little kiosk finally opened on her next.

She dropped the ritualistic opening lines and went right to the issue at hand. "Father, since they've taken Tavish away, Michal insists that I stop teaching. His fear is that our street will be filled with gendarmes, and I too will be carted away. I can't give up on my students Father."

"And what is it you want from me?"

"Father the basement of the church is very large, almost like the catacombs. We could meet there; if you're amenable?"

"Leona, you put the church at great risk. This is not something I can answer to immediately. Allow me some time to mull this over," a long pause, "I'll get back to you."

# CHAPTER 9

He hoped he had it timed right. The guard from the midnight shift would still be on duty, lethargic and groggy from another night of sleepless inactivity. Delivery traffic through the checkpoints slowed down after two in the morning.

Dysthmus honked his horn and waited for the guard to appear on the loading dock.

"Guten tag," He said as he climbed out of his cab, with his clipboard under his arm.

"What is so important for you to be here at this hour?"

"An urgent delivery, arms to be loaded on the train to Poznan." He handed the guard the clipboard.

This could take only a few minutes. The guard appeared relieved; he wouldn't have to examine the freight. The flyer, alerting inspectors of the new label, along with instructions on proper procedure, had already made the rounds of the stations. He signed the document, tore off the voucher under the perforated line and waved Dysthmus on his way.

Business in town was in its early morning flux. The birds were swooping down to scavenge whatever debris was left on the streets. The tantalizing aroma of fresh baked bread from the legitimate and illicit bakeries that filled the city set his stomach to grumbling. He parked his truck in front of a building on Napoleon Square, hopped out of the vehicle and walked over to the grated cellar door that was set into the pavement for deliveries. He lifted the handle to pull the door open, closed it behind him, and scrambled down the stairs that emptied into a dark cavern.

His flashlight lit the way through the maze of corridors, until he came to a concealed door in the wall, distinguishable only to those who knew where to look for the small cross that was carved on its surface. Using the butt of his flashlight, he rapped out his special code and waited, longer than necessary. He rapped again, after several minutes, Stash, the bleary-eyed proprietor of the illicit still answered the knock.

"You here to pick up a delivery?"

"No, I'm here to sell you some grain to make liquor." He slid through the narrow opening that Stash had allowed. There, in a windowless room, sat a bubbling contraption; the fumes alone, carried a staggering effect.

Dysthmus opened his hand to expose the quality of grain he had brought in as a sample. Stash took a pinch of the stuff, sniffed it, and tasted the sample. He made no reaction.

"How much, at what cost?"

He gave him a quote, and Stash gave a reaction.

"You're crazy! That's grain, not gold!"

"Take it or leave it." He turned to go. "I'm off to the black-market bakers. They won't haggle."

"Wait, the price will cut into my profit." A strained look pulled at his face. "Be reasonable."

Stash wanted a twenty-five percent cut; they settled on twelve percent.

Dysthmus unloaded most of the grain for Stash's liquor production. A few sacks remained. There were over two-hundred illicit bakers in and around town. Most of them were black market. They had been giving away free bread to their starving neighbors since the war began. The inflated prices they charged to the wealthy Germans absorbed the cost. The last sacks of grain would be a donation. The Home Army was hard pressed for funds; the zlotys gained from Stash would go into their coffers.

Michal Bednarek decided to have lunch at his usual stop, a café in the center of Warsaw. Most of the professionals in town gathered there because it served a decent cup of coffee, thanks to black market purveyors.

The server was occupied, and Bednarek was trying to catch her eye. He glanced at the copy of the underground newspaper, *Poland's Journal*. While he waited for service, he searched the pages for his favorite column. Zygmunt Kaminski, the editor, offered a weekly column which usually contained zany tongue-in-cheek aphorisms. So far, these satirical articles had escaped the Germans' censure. Many of the underground newspapers were mailed to the Gestapo, usually with a message of the latest disruption by the partisans. Often with a brazen comment like, "We thought you'd like to know..."

Michal smiled in amusement when the very man himself walked in the door. He raised his hand to catch his attention.

"Kaminski, come join me."

His friend waved in recognition and added a 'wait' signal with his hand. He wrapped his arm around the server's waist and whispered in her ear.

Kaminski was quite a few years younger than Michal. Short and portly, he carried his weight in a robust manner. His well-tailored suit and expensive hat set him apart from most of the professionals surviving in Warsaw. A carnation filled the buttonhole of his lapel.

After nodding 'hello' and addressing several other people, whom he seemed to know quite well, Kaminski made his way to the table.

"Bednarek, I haven't seen you around lately."

"I've been busy. I was just getting ready to read your column. I could use a little light hearted humor today."

"You won't find it in my column, Michael. They've arrested the father of the party."

"I saw the arrest from my living room window. Afterwards, I ran over to Szucha Street and had a chat with Stroop, which got me absolutely nowhere."

Kaminski appeared surprised by this report. "You stuck your neck out, Michal?"

"So, it seems, but I was only performing my duty as a lawyer, and I told that to Stroop."

"We think he's been taken to Pawiak Prison."

The server approached the table and Kaminski once again turned on the charm. "You remember Magda Odkowska, first lady of the stage of Warsaw." He took her hand and kissed it. "She is still my first love."

Michal blinked in disbelief. He did remember her, fondly, but the change in her appearance was so drastic, he found it difficult to believe it was she. They placed their order. The aged actress rewarded them with a sweet smile accompanied by a slight bow, and then she ambled off in the direction of the kitchen.

"Oh, my God, Zygmunt, it's hard to believe she was once the queen of the stage."

"Life's been hard on her since the occupation. She was lucky to find this job. She takes her meals here and she pays for her room and other needs with the pay and tips she makes."

"Remind me to leave a larger than usual tip."

Kaminski returned to the earlier conversation. "We are trying to ascertain if Tavish indeed is in Paviak. We plan to remove him and get him to a safe-haven." He looked directly into Michal's eyes. "You have a huge network of important people to draw from. If you come across any information, you must let me know."

Michal nodded, and from the absence of any look of agreement on his friend's face, Kaminski took it to mean that this was not a source he could depend on. Nevertheless, he pushed further. No intelligent Pole could avoid the pervading conflict for long.

"Do you still hold your offices in Napoleon Square, Michael?"

"Yes, I do."

"Very well, I'll stop by to see you, in the event you may come up with some pertinent news on your longtime friend and neighbor, Tavish."

# CHAPTER 10

Father Lipinski was at his usual post after mass on Sunday. His greeting to Bednarek seemed warmer than usual. Michal had sought him out for a brief consultation after his meeting with Kaminski, which had left him with a gray feeling of guilt. Lipinski, ever the diplomat, did not offer any valid suggestions, nevertheless, Michal rationalized that he was in the right, and went away with a feeling that the priest had done him some good. Lipinski never mentioned Leona's furtive request for use of the church basement.

"You seem to be dealing with your recent irritation, Michal."

"Yes, Father." Was the priest picking at a scab?

"Ah, Leona, we have only three more Fridays for Stations of the Cross. I am expecting to see you there," he issued a knowing look, "mention it to your friends."

Leona beamed a smile and kissed his hand. "Thank you, Father, I'll be there."

After breakfast, Leona and Irena lingered over coffee and Kaminski's Journal. Janina was busy in the kitchen and Michal had gone into his study to work on a client's books.

"Irena, I have arranged to conduct class in the church basement. The arrangement is temporary, at best, only three weeks, but it's a start and Lipinski may come up with a more permanent schedule."

"What a relief. I'd much rather complete your course in a class, with other students. What about other classes?" She quickly identified the class that held her interest. "A friend of mine is looking for classes in Architecture. So far there doesn't seem to be one."

"Just now, I cannot speak to any other classes that Father might be willing to accommodate."

They heard the phone ring in Michal's study. A muffled initial greeting, and then a louder tone climaxed by a ringing off.

Irena looked to her mother, who merely shrugged her shoulders.

Michal entered the room in a somewhat agitated mood. "I'm sorry I ever bumped into Kaminski. He's made an appointment to see me at my office."

"Why should this disturb you, Michal? I thought he was a friend of yours."

"He's not coming to see me in friendship, Leona!"

"Tata, you're unusually upset about this. It may just be a meeting to discuss a legal issue. He's involved in so many projects."

Michal stormed out of the room. "I know what issue it is he wants to discuss, and it is definitely not legal."

Janina came to clear away the coffee cups. "Is there something wrong with Pan?"

"No, not exactly Janina, it's just the usual annoyance involved with legal matters."

After mass on Monday, Leona invited Father Lipinski to breakfast with her at the Center Café, where they served the good black-market coffee. He eagerly agreed.

Mid-morning on a Monday posed no difficulty in obtaining service. The ex-actress, Magda, was at their table before they were properly seated. Leona ordered coffee for them while the priest looked through the breakfast menu.

Magda served the coffee and asked Lipinski for a blessing before she took their order.

Leona reached across the table and touched the priest's hand. "Thank you, Father. I wasn't sure you'd come through for me."

"Leona, higher education is very important. It's almost three years since Hitler shut down the universities and secondary schools. You know—you've been teaching clandestine classes in your home all this time."

"Yes, very much against Michal's concerns. This episode with Tavish has exacerbated all of his trepidations. There is no way he will allow me to continue."

"Well, you have the northwest corner of the basement for these next three Fridays. You may contact your students, and if you like, I'll include an embedded message in my sermon this week, in the event there may be a potential history major at mass this Sunday."

"Thank you, Father, I never expected this much support."

"After Lent, we shall launch a study of Revelations on Wednesday evenings. This will be announced during services and in the church bulletin for the next three weeks. I know that piece of scripture will glean a large audience." He lowered his head, but not before she caught the conspiratorial smile on his face. "The northwest corner, of course, will be available to you."

There was a time, directly after the occupation, when Bednarek thought he would not be able to survive. There was no longer any need for the services of a lawyer; no one could afford legal fees. Michal was one of the few attorneys who continued practicing on a *pro-bono* basis, not only as a service to the citizens of Warsaw, but also to keep his hands in the practice of law.

Fortunately, his attempt to earn a living by serving the Schindlerites as an accountant paid off well enough to cover his expenses. The office on Napoleon Square still retained the top-shelf character of the former lucrative years. The comfortable chairs and the wet bar remained intact. Gone was the attractive female staff to cater to his client's needs. A part time secretary kept his paper work and correspondence in order.

He arrived at his office precisely at eight o'clock. Kaminski was waiting at the door.

"Good morning, Michal." He handed him the latest 'BI,' the daily Information Bulletin of the Home Army, which was refused.

"What is this urgency, Zygmunt? I am unable to give legal advice to conspirators."

Michal turned the key in the latch and opened the door. Kaminski was right behind him.

"I'm not looking for legal advice. Consider this an occasion to enjoy a casual chat with an old friend. I know that you have high regard for old friendships, Michal."

The journalist boldly took a seat, while Bednarek hovered over him, visibly annoyed. Kaminski drew a notepad from the pocket in his vest and read his notes aloud. "The Polish Communist Party is boasting of its recent diversionary action. A team of them were involved in a botched operation yesterday. One of them threw a hand-grenade into a window of the Nectar, where some German soldiers sat drinking beer." He looked up at Michal, who displayed mild interest in the story. He replaced the notepad in his pocket. "The commies never consider the consequences of their disruptive tactics. The gendarmes filled the street in no time and shot aimlessly into the crowds that had gathered. As far as I know, the team got away without losing a member and reported their successful assault to their commander."

Kaminski looked up at Michal and presented a large grin. "Have I caught your attention, Michal?"

The attorney bristled. "Look here, Zygmunt, I have a good deal of work ahead of me for the day, and I am not overjoyed with the prospects of engaging in casual conversation. This is neither the time nor the place."

"I'll catch you at lunch one day. Meanwhile, here are some items of interest to not only you, but to all good Poles."

He dropped the Information Bulletin on the desk and saw himself out the door.

Michal glanced at the first page. Obviously, Kaminski had underlined, in red, the items of interest, Szucha Street and Paviak Prison. He knew the reputation of the II Bulletin. It was the official organ of the Home Army's Bureau of Information and Propaganda. He dropped it in the waste basket. Attorney, Michal Bednarek, had no time for underground intrigue.

# CHAPTER 11

One of Kaminski's important stops was the Office of Labor. He kept the office supplied with the proper paper products necessary for working certificates, as well as letter heads for official documents. Weights, color, and watermarks were constantly changing under order of the Gestapo in their effort to stay ahead of the underground forgery system.

Joseph Adamski's *Ausbeis* noted him as a *Volksdeutscher*, Manager of Office of Labor. Before the war, Adamski had been an attorney at law in the Court of Poland. Samuel Tannenbaum was his legal name. Immediately after the German occupation, Tannenbaum went into hiding and joined the Warsaw resistance group. The Home Army provided him with flawless identification documents. His code name for underground activities was 'Aaron.'

Zegota was the code name for the Council of Aid to the Jews. It operated under the auspices of Premier Sikorski and the Government in Exile. It was founded in 1942 by the Government Delegation in Warsaw, who witnessed the relentless persecution of the Jews. The Nazi edict of deportation, which began in July of that year, was the determining factor for government intervention. The organization provided food, medical care, relief money, and false identity documents for Jews hiding within the 'Aryan' side of occupied Warsaw.

The SS began rounding up Jews from Warsaw and the surrounding suburbs in April of 1940. Governor General Frank managed to crowd four hundred thousand Jews into a square mile and a half within an active business section of Warsaw. The virulent anti-Semitist, Joseph Goebbels, Nazi Propaganda Minister, made sure they were contained by ordering a wall to surround them. The Ghetto became a cage within a cage. Construction of a nine-foot wall, topped with barbed wire that began in October was completed in mid-November of 1940. Those who escaped took on Aryan identities with forged documents.

The ZOB, another faction of Zegota was initiated by Jewish youth groups. They recognized the fact that Hitler intended to annihilate the Jews from the face of the earth. The group made several ineffective starts to form their own militia, and finally offered their services to the High Command of the Home Army, where they received training, arms and munitions. Aaron was the facilitator for the communication network between Zegota and the ZOB.

Kaminski stepped into the Office of Labor, just before noon, under the pretext of recruiting a part time clerk for his office.

"Pan Adamski, I didn't realize how close we are to the lunch hour." He looked up at the clock on the wall. "Where are you having lunch, today?"

"Here. I brought a pail."

"Join me. I hate to eat alone. Save the pail for tomorrow."

Kaminski knew the storm clouds were gathering over the Ghetto. He was gathering information for an article. He began to interview Adamski as they walked toward the restaurant.

"How close are they?"

"It looks like the night of Passover, April 19."

"How are they fixed for ammunition and weapons?"

"The minimum. The Home Army is providing them with all that they can, but they also have plans, and they can't deplete their stock." He lowered his voice, "The ZOB have been stockpiling weapons and ammunition, since the first draft of deportation last year. They have used ingenious methods of getting the stuff into the Ghetto; through cellars of adjoining houses, through the sewers, and gaps torn into the walls. They also know the safe places within the Ghetto where they keep the weapons stored."

They arrived at the Schilling and chose a booth that was surrounded by German entrepreneurs. The Schindlerites paid them no mind. Matters of business and finance were being discussed.

Kaminski continued the interview.

"What, would you say, is the participation rate among the residents?"

"Most of the elders are compliant under the Nazi rule. They are the sheep, who are resigned to the situation. The elite believe, because of their status, that they will be treated well by the Nazis. The Ghetto Police are in total denial. They believe they are indispensable to the Reich. Commitment and courage comes from the young. They know that the entire population will be annihilated, and the Ghetto will be destroyed. They choose to fight, knowing that in the end all will die."

Kaminski didn't take notes. The narrative was too compelling. He would never forget the images Aaron had drawn for him. A loud murmur filled the dining room; it seemed as if something of vital importance had occurred.

Kaminski motioned to the waitress, a known partisan, "Helcha, what's going on?"

"Pan, have you heard? It's all over town. The Germans are accusing the Russians of the mass murder of Poles—someplace in Smolensk."

Kaminski nodded his head, "Katyn."

# CHAPTER 12

The courthouse that Michal served pro-bono one day a week was situated on the line that divided the city from the Jewish Ghetto. He approached the building from the Aryan side and made his way up the stairs to the third-floor courtroom. Only cases pertaining to civil matters involving Poles were heard in this particular room. Cases involving the General Government and the civil justice of the German population were heard in a separate court.

At the top of the stairs, Michal recognized a former colleague standing in the hall. It was quite some time since he last saw the man and his appearance was drastically changed. He remembered him as a rather portly sort of fellow. He appeared gaunt and older than his years.

"Steinberg, how have you been?" He advanced toward him.

The man failed to acknowledge him; he remained staring out the window that faced the Ghetto. An uproar of growing proportions was resonating through the window. The weather was moderate enough for the window to be opened, yet it and the other windows in the building remained closed. The stench from the Ghetto was intolerable. The Nazis had imposed a cost on burials, an onus the residents could ill afford. They resorted to stripping the bodies of their family members and leaving them on a pile to provide anonymity.

Michal could hear the voices of the men, women, and children resounding from the street below. The loudest voices heard were those of the SS men who were shouting out orders.

"Schnell! Schnell! The Germans were using their rifle butts to shuttle their victims onto a ramp. Some of the weaker, and older folk were unable to keep pace and stumbled and fell. This caused the others, who were following them to lose their footing and create a pile-up. The slowdown of the march incited the Germans who raised their guns and shot randomly into the pile. They then forced those standing nearby to push the bodies off the ramp.

Steinberg spoke, his voice a monotone, "We are down to seventy thousand lives in the Ghetto. The soldiers are collecting people for the death camp in Treblinka. It's been a while since the last deportation,"

Michal was unable to respond. He put his hand on Steinberg's shoulder. One of the magistrates had left the courtroom and walked over to them. There were tears in his eyes.

"We are totally isolated. No one in the world seems to care what is happening. Is there no humanity left?"

Steinberg took Michal's hand, "I have been living on the outside, on forged papers of a *Volksdeutsche*. It's time I went home." He gave a gentle squeeze to the hand he held, "Goodbye, Bednarek, I'll not be seeing you again."

Michal had no heart to return to his office. He wandered aimlessly through the streets until he came upon Malakowski Square. Fat buds were appearing on the rhododendron bushes and tulips were flooding the square in a vibrant carpet of colors. He sat on a bench and tried to absorb some of the tranquility of the verdant spring display. He watched the people enjoying the weather and the flowers with a feeling of surrealism. Children were laughing and chasing one another about as the old people sat on the benches, enjoying the show. It all seemed out of sync with reality. There was a normalcy to their behavior. Normalcy within an occupied and restricted city? Yet, compared with the scene at the courthouse, the spectacle on display in Malakowski Square did provide an element of normalcy. These people could still hope for an end to their struggle, and even imagine the possibility of a future beyond. The Jews were left with nothing. His gut reacted as though a bomb had imploded within his soul. There was a deep and dark void at the seat of his emotions.

He found himself walking in the direction of Kaminski's favorite waterhole. Would he be there at this time of day? He looked at his watch, three-forty, it was possible.

A man and a woman sat at a table by the window. They held hands and looked lovingly at one another; considering the time and place, it may well have been a convenient tryst. She smiled up at him and he was gently rubbing her hand. Michal took no notice of the engaging couple; his attention was focused on the lone patron sitting at the end of the bar. Kaminski raised his hand in greeting to acknowledge Michal's presence while he continued his conversation he held with the bartender.

Michal climbed onto the barstool next to him and ordered a double vodka. Kaminski stopped mid-sentence and raised an eyebrow, "Isn't this a bit early for you?"

Michal waited until his drink was in front of him to speak. He downed it in one gulp.

"They are taking the Jews to the slaughter house."

Kaminski motioned for a refill.

"I've just finished speaking with a dead man. A man I studied law with. A Jew, bound for Treblinka."

The bartender retreated and Kaminski murmured. "The Jews are preparing for an uprising. They have nothing to lose."

"When?"

"In the next few days. It will be a massacre. There is a great deal of heroism in their final suicidal effort."

He was struck by the obvious pain in Michal's eyes. Unable to provide any comfort, He offered a challenge instead. "Michal, you can no longer sit on the fence. Civil Resistance needs you."

"Me, what could I do? I have no heart for insurgence."

"You could serve in your profession. The Secret Court could use you."

# CHAPTER 13

Friday evening Michal was faced with eating dinner alone.

"They are at church for the Stations." Janina informed him.

He picked through the meal, poured a tumbler of vodka, and withdrew to his study.

Leona was evasive when she got home. It was well after Stations, just before curfew, when she and Irena slipped in the front door. Michal confronted her, but she brushed him off.

"It is more important than ever that we do penance and prayer. You too need to pray more."

He let the incident slide to avoid a serious argument. He was sure that she had found a way to continue teaching, and he was certain that Father Lipinski had a hand in the curriculum.

The following week Michal arrived at his office at his usual time; he unlocked the door and gathered the mail from its box on the wall. Tucked directly under the lid, on top of the pile, was a copy of Poland's Journal. He looked up and down the street, expecting to see Kaminski hovering nearby. This hand-delivered issue was hot off the press. The Journal was a weekly publication that made its appearance in town on Thursdays.

He managed his office alone. Tessa, his former secretary, came to the office twice a week to copy and collate his documents. She maintained his files and typed his correspondence. A quick review of the documents she typed the night before seemed in order. He flicked through the mail, separating the important looking addresses from the trivial. Poland's Journal was placed in his desk drawer; he was expecting a client.

He put the pot on to perk before Herr Klaufer arrived for his appointment. Klaufer owned several businesses in Warsaw, and occasionally had issues with Polish citizens. He had an annoying habit of trying to pick Michael's brain for answers to his legal disputes free of charge.

Klaufer entered the office before Michal had a chance to open one of the important envelopes.

"Good morning, Bednarek."

"Good morning." He wasn't ready for him. Klaufer's appointment was for eight-thirty, another twenty minutes away.

"One moment, Herr Klaufer, I've just arrived, and I have yet to pull your file."

"Don't rush. Have you read the newspaper?" He handed him the *Nowy Kourier*.

"Not as yet. It's my practice to read it over lunch."

Klaufer held out the front page. Two headlines competed for attention:

## MASS GRAVES DISCOVERED IN FOREST OF KATYN
## POLISH GOVERNMENT IN EXILE
## DEMANDS INVESTIGATION

His professional reserve was punctured. He tried to recover a neutral façade but realized his attempt to cover up only verified the shock he felt. A twisted smile appeared on Klaufer's face.

"Well, I leave you to peruse the paper during your lunch hour." He laid the paper on the desk.

Michal excused himself while he went for Klaufer's books. He had pushed his financial expertise to the limit. The books balanced.

Klaufer laid a finger to his lips and nodded his head in approval. The clever manipulation of numbers showed a generous profit within the confines of the mandated tax structure. The figures were indisputable.

"You seem to have proceedings in order, Pan Bednarek." He left with that patronizing smile of his. "Good day to you, and I hope to see you at the cinema."

Citizens of Warsaw held a boycott over the German operated cinemas and entertainment venues. Anyone caught attending a German event was considered a collaborator. When the former manager of the theater signed a contract with the Germans to continue at his post, the secret court accused him of collaboration and rendered a sentence of retribution. He was shot on the street in front of the box office. Michal would not be going to the cinema.

When he was sure that Klaufer was well on his way, he locked the door and grabbed the *Nowy Kourier*. Under the headline announcing mass murders in Katyn, he was horrified to read that between March and April of 1940, the NKVD, the Soviet intelligence operation under the department of Internal Affairs, had murdered over 22,000 of the Polish elite. Lavrenti Beria chief of the bureau had ordered the massacre, and Stalin had signed the document. The victims had been incarcerated in the Kozelsk Prisoner of War Camp, not far from Smolensk, Russia.

In bold type was an advertisement:

Film, Soviet Massacre of Polish Officers, shown at the Cinema Warszawa, all this week.

Under the second heading:

## IN EXILE POLISH GOVERNMENT
## DEMANDS INVESTIGATION

The article reported the reaction of the Polish Exiled Government in London. The news had gravely impacted the entire staff. Premier Sikorski appealed to the International Red Cross for an investigation to verify the indictment against the Soviets.

Michal had an impulse to contact Kaminski for validation, but he was too emotionally upset to continue in this vein. Poland's Journal remained in his desk drawer. He would attack the underground press tomorrow, and maybe get in touch with the messenger. His greater impulse was to get home to Leona, who seemed to be more in touch with the reality of life under oppression than he was. It would seem that she had every reason to defy his edict to stop teaching.

Janina was approaching the apartment with grocery packages in her arms just as Michal turned up the street. From the number of bags she juggled, it must have been a good day at the black market. He hurried his step to catch up with her.

"Here, Janina let me help you." He plucked two packages from her tight grip and appreciated the look of relief that showed on her face.

"Thank you, Pan. You're home early tonight."

"Yes, I worked through lunch. Is Pani Leona at home?"

"She's been working in her office all day. I have a special treat for her. I baked a plum cake for desert."

"That is special."

They unloaded the packages in the kitchen and Michal went directly to his wife's study.

"Michal, what are you doing home?"

"I rushed through my day." He sheepishly approached the desk and kissed her head.

"Grading papers, I see."

She put her pen down and swiveled the chair around to face him. There was a look of contrition on her face. Evidently, she had been at this project all day, and had not heard the horrific news of Katyn.

He found her demeanor touching. He knelt down beside her. "It's alright, dear. It would be just as ridiculous to ask the roses not to bud. I know your dedication to your work, but that leaves me with a great concern for your welfare."

She put her arms around his neck. "I'll be very careful, and you'll just have to trust God to get us through this horror. Please, Michal, don't work so hard at controlling things."

There was no need to bring a much-needed moment of healing to a close. He released her arms from around his neck and took her hands, "Come, we didn't say goodnight in a proper manner last night."

# CHAPTER 14

Michal was rushing up Napoleon Square to his office without an umbrella to shield him from the heavy downpour. From the corner of his eye, he caught the image of a man taking large swift steps toward him. His head was hunched between his shoulders; he also was without an umbrella. He recognized that solid body wrapped in a wind jacket topped with a large, brimmed hat. Kaminski was headed in his direction; no doubt to confront him about the latest issue of Poland's Journal that he had left behind.

Michal ran the last few steps to open his office door. He scooped up the paper from his desk and gave a quick perusal to satisfy his persistent friend that he had not ignored his effort. He glanced through the article that was boldly circled with red ink.

Ignatz Tavish, former Member of Parliament, has been seized by the Gestapo and is being held in Paviak Prison. The prison is notorious for swift executions and quick dispersal of all who enter there.

Kaminski was at the door before he could lay the paper down, but Michal had a working knowledge of the article.

"Bednarek, I'm in time. I saw you rushing out of the rain."

"Good morning, Zygmunt," the usual undertone of irritation was conspicuous by its absence, "please have a seat. Would you like a cup of coffee?"

Kaminski was faced with having to adjust his manner to this unexpected civility. "Yes, Please." He removed his hat and opened his jacket. He picked up the newspaper, still unfolded, and took a seat.

Michal caught the action, "No, I haven't read the whole paper, just the article on Tavish."

He took the seat across from Kaminski, so he could view him face to face, without a desk between them.

Kaminski began, "Michal, we cannot leave the father of the party in the hands of the Nazis. He did not live his whole life for his people only to end up being tortured to death." He looked unwaveringly into Michal's eyes and was surprised when his friend did not flinch.

The coffee was briskly perking on the hot plate and Michal excused himself.

After he poured and served the coffee, Michal changed the subject to the Katyn incident.

"A client of mine, a Herr Klaufer, brought me the *Nowy Kourier* with a story of a massacre in Katyn."

"Ah, yes, unfortunately, the Nazis scooped me. That is because they are the ones to uncover the bodies."

"Is it true?"

"We don't know. We are holding that story in abeyance pending further investigation."

"Yes, there was an accompanying article that reported Premier Sikorski, in London, is seeking affirmation from the International Red Cross."

A look of instant epiphany lit up Kaminski's face. "Michal, I am about to ask you to do something so bold and out of character for you. Please listen, and do not answer quickly."

Michal examined Kaminski's face as if to try to discern the question before he asked it, in the event he would be caught off guard and acquiesce.

"Michal, the courier from London, Zamski, will be here next week. I was going to interview him, but that may be stretching my neck too far."

"Zygmunt, what is your point?"

"You are considered a non-entity in the field of conspirators. Michal, you would make the perfect contact person to get the story."

"You're crazy! I have no skill at intrigue."

"You have the skill of a barrister; a barrister beyond suspicion. You must do this. We have enough to do with Tavish in Paviak and Piekalkiewicz on Szucha Street"

Michal got an image of Tavish, a man whom he loved and respected all his life, being dragged from his longtime home on Zielona Street with blood streaming down his face. He would never forget the look on Steinberg's face at the court house and Leona marking her student's papers last night.

He breathed a deep sigh. "What is it you would have me do, Zygmunt?"

Too much 'history' was going on in the daily lives of Professor Bednarek's Wednesday evening class. The news of Katyn was wide spread, and this evening's meeting afforded them a chance to vent their fears and concerns.

After dismissal, some of the students remained to address a specific issue they had. Irena, sat with a friend of hers at the back of the room, waiting for the others to leave. Leona had her eye on the curfew and hurried her students along.

"What is it dear? We really must leave."

"Mamma, this is Rihard Borowski, he's the student I told you about; the one who is looking to take up classes in architecture."

Borowski was rail thin; he wore steel rimmed glasses and had the look of a serious bookworm. It was apparent that he was shy, and Leona realized just what it was that Irena found so appealing in him. He was like a lost puppy and Irena had a strong nurturing instinct.

She beamed a smile his way and extended her hand to him. "Pleased to meet you, Rihard. Irena has been most earnest in advocating for you."

"Thank you, Professor, you're most gracious. I've had an interest in architecture before I could pronounce the word. I was captured on my first visit to the Royal Castle in Warsaw, and I've never been set free."

"Charming," she loosened her hand from his grip, "Then we must arrange a time for a meeting."

She looked at her daughter. "Irena, you must check with Janina and come up with an evening when we can get together over dinner to discuss this matter."

She deposited her books into Rihard's hands and tucked her hand into the crook of his arm. "Come we must leave. Father wants to close the church."

After the emotion filled evening with her class, Leona felt the need to unwind.

"Irena, I'm going to heat up some chocolate. Would you like to join me?"

"No, Mama, but save some for Tata, he loves chocolate. I'm going to take a bath and go to bed. The evening was much too stimulating for me." She gave her mother a kiss on the cheek. "Thank you for being so kind to Rihard this evening, Mama."

"Who could help being kind to Rihard? He's so—bookish, and so needy." She gave a gentle smack to her daughter's bottom. "Good night, Laletchka." She watched her tall, willowy daughter walk to the hall.

One of the local artists had offered to paint a portrait of Irena when she was only ten years old. "Her coloring is incredible; she has eyes that appear to be turquoise, her skin is ivory, and her hair, never have I seen such a rich shade of brown."

Irena was in full bloom. She had much to offer to life. Warm and bright, she possessed a genuine compassion for others. Who knew how her life would play out during the struggles of a war that seemed to have no end in sight?

She went into the kitchen to pull out a pot to heat the milk. She heard Michal at the door.

"Leona, is that you in the kitchen?"

"Yes, I'm making chocolate. Wash up and I'll pour you a cup."

He walked over to the music cabinet and selected a favorite Chopin and placed it on the gramophone before going to the bathroom.

The music played softly as they relaxed in their favorite chairs and sipped the warm brew.

"How did this evening's class go?"

"Not as good as my future ones – I hope. They were just too excited. The news of Katyn has all of Warsaw upset. In fact, more people than usual showed up for Father's lecture this evening. I'm sure they were seeking reassurance and comfort from Lipinski."

She cocked her head; Michal seemed distracted, preoccupied.

"Is something bothering you, Michal?"

He sighed heavily. "Kaminski has wheedled me into a compromising situation – and I'm afraid he's not through with me."

"Whatever do you mean?"

He recounted his meeting with Kaminski. "He has managed to recruit me to interview a courier from the Government in Exile about the Katyn Massacre."

"Michal," there was more than concern in her voice; "you can't do that! You have no skill in intrigue, nor do you want to be involved. What if you get caught?"

"What if? What if Kaminski gets caught? What if the courier gets caught?" He reached over to touch her hand. "Most importantly, Leona, what if you get caught?"

She sighed and covered his hand with hers. "I suppose you're right, Michal. We must all try to do our best to upset the Germans in any way we can." She released his hand and reached for her cup.

"And what did you mean when you said that Kaminski is not through with you?"

"I'm sure he will lure me into yet another act of conspiracy. Once the mouse nibbles on the cheese, the trap is set."

# CHAPTER 15

Late in the afternoon on Thursday, Kaminski dropped by Michal's office with a copy of the latest issue of Poland's Journal.

"We picked up the story from the Nowy Kurier."

Michal read the headline on the first page.

## KATYN GRAVESITE UNCOVERED

The article went on to state that graves, presumed to be those of Polish Officers and noted intelligencia were discovered in the Katyn Forest. The Germans reported the incident, claiming the exhumed bodies were those of prisoners held by the Soviets in the Kozelsk Prisoner of War Camp near Smolensk, Russia.

Further investigation is warranted. Premier Sikorski has demanded an investigation be conducted by the International Red Cross to verify the report.

"What do you think, Zygmunt, was it the Germans?"

"Knowing the hatred that Stalin harbors for Poland, I assure you, it was the Russians." He made a brisk turn toward the door.

"I have to run. My real mission was to prepare you for your meeting with Zamski, tomorrow morning at eight o'clock at the Napoleon Café."

"Zygmunt! What will I say? How shall I know him?"

"He's tall, well-built and bald. Just take a legal pad along and conduct a deposition." He turned on his heel and walked out the door.

Bednarek's stress level revealed itself in the iron grip he held on to his brief case. He convinced himself that he was presenting his usual urbane demeanor as he turned the corner of Warecki Street to approach the café. He noticed a tall man emerging from a dark green German Opel Kapitan. The man wore a stylish felt hat, which hid the one distinguishing feature given to him by Zygmunt. Michal neared the entrance to the café and slipped through the door to observe the man further.

Once inside, he kept his eye on the door as he hovered by the coat rack. Presently, the man in question walked through the doorway and removed his hat. He was bald, but his appearance did not match the image of the bald-headed man Michal had conjured in his mind. He was a youthful, handsome man, despite his premature balding. He had the physique of an athlete, and he was extremely well dressed. He walked toward the coat rack.

"Guten Morgen, Herr Schtingle, I am Michal Bednarek," he extended his hand in a formal greeting, "I'm representing your firm in the legal issue involving funding."

"Guten Morgen." He reported in a clear baritone voice.

Michal led the way to a table near the kitchen, which was usually the last one to be filled. He felt very much like the hero in a film of intrigue. How had he managed to come up with that name, Schtingle? They settled in with coffee and Michal pulled out his legal pad and pen, ready to take his deposition.

"What can you tell me to clarify the report?"

"I can vouch for its accuracy," he lowered his voice to an audible whisper, "I could be lying in that gravesite."

Michal caught his breath as he pretended to be writing down the statement.

Zamski continued, maintaining a low tone, "I was an NCO in the Polish Army at the time of the invasion. Fortunately, for me, I was fighting on the western border when the Soviet Army converged with the German Army in September of thirty-nine. The officer in charge of our company appraised the situation as two of our mortal enemies reaching toward each other to capture us in the middle like a vice. He commanded us to retreat to the outskirts of the town. Once we had caught our bearings, we joined other retreating soldiers who fled to the forest. Many of those bodies lying in the graves of Katyn were my colleagues who were taken prisoners that day, by the Russians."

"Is there any information of the number of those interred?"

"The mass murders were conducted by the NKVD, under direct orders from the bureau's chief, Lavrenti Beria, with Stalin's full approval. I have conferred with the Polish Secretary of the International Red Cross. The total estimate is twenty-two thousand souls; eight-thousand Polish Officers, six-thousand Police Officers, and the other eight-thousand were members of the elite; the public officials, medical personnel, educators, and scientists."

Michal had scribbled down the figures and assigned a monetary value to them in keeping with his fictitious legal case. He had a hard time looking up from his pad to meet Zamski's eyes.

"I am so sorry for your personal experiences in this tragedy."

"It has provided me with a fearless approach to carry out my mission. I thank God for my life and my ability to participate."

The tables began to fill with patrons being served breakfast. The two men briefly touched on the recent announcement by the SS on the death of Piekalkiewicz, the official head of the underground government, which K-Division had not been able to resolve.

They finished their coffee, Zamski picked up the check and palmed a slip of paper into Michal's hand as they said goodbye.

Michal felt a surge of pride as he watched Zamski walk out the door of the café. He was aware of a struggle within himself as he tried to separate pride from a new feeling of commitment. He waited until he was out on the street, a good distance from the cafe, before he glanced at the slip of paper in his hand. It was a note containing instructions on how to contact the courier via the underground radio waves. Michal now possessed the accurate details for an article for Kaminski, and call letters to an underground radio station where he could contact Zamski in the future.

Two magnetic shields were temporarily affixed to the front doors of a dark green Opel Kapitan, each bearing the Nazi swastika. Attached to the antennae flew a small flag, also sporting a swastika. The car approached the Central Station in Warsaw and the driver, dressed in the uniform of a German Sergeant, hopped out of the car and ceremoniously opened the door for his passenger, a Wehrmacht General, carrying an attaché case. The high-ranking officer returned the sergeant's salute with a click of his heels. He turned to make his way to the station just as a fashionably dressed young woman walked in front of him. He smiled broadly and tipped his cap, exposing his bald head. The General continued on his way to the station master's window to pick up his first-class ticket to Poznan.

# CHAPTER 16

Kaminski's timing was precise, as usual. Michal had just returned to his office after his breakfast with Zamski, when Kaminski made his entrance.

"Have you copy for my next edition?"

Michal responded with an amused grin and a nod of his head. "You are punctual!" He opened his valise and pulled out his legal pad with the notations of his conversation with the courier.

"I have a deadline to keep." Kaminski plucked a handful of peppermints from the dish on Michal's desk and took a seat.

"Here are the statistics on the Katyn massacre, twenty-two thousand all told. Zamski told me a chilling personal story. He said he was an NCO during the first siege of 1939. He was serving under a commander who was wise enough to know that his men were cornered between the advancing forces of Germans from the west and the Red Army from the east. The commander ordered retreat. If it were not for that, Zamski would be lying in Katyn along with his fellow-officers who were captured by the Red's and sent to Smolensk."

"He's a silent hero. He's known as a courier, but in fact, he is one of the best espionage agents under Churchill's Special Operations Executive, the SOE."

"I was very impressed with him. Tell me Zygmunt, how long has this massacre been privileged information with the Nazis?"

"They've known for some time. Don't forget, the Soviets and Germans were allies in September of '39', when they coordinated the invasion against Poland. That's when Russia took the prisoners for Smolensk. The Germans held it under their hats until it could do the most damage. Goebbels chose to disclose it now in the light of the increasing stature Stalin is gaining with the British and the Americans."

Michal sniggered, "Then this heinous disclosure should cause a definite rift between Russia and the West."

"Not so. Britain has a file confirming Russia's guilt, but the pro-soviet majority of the British government buries its head in the sand. They would rather believe the Germans were the murderers. Stalin is digging in his heels to involve himself with the Grand Alliance, and Poland is currently lying in a basket on the doorstep. It remains to be seen if the Western Allies will play foster parents or toss us to the Soviets."

"Are the Western Allies that gullible?"

"It's politics, Michal. The Red Army is a powerful force. When the time comes, they are in perfect position to crush the Germans on their march west, over Poland. The whole situation bodes no good for Poland, under any circumstances. This sudden disclosure has caused Stalin to distance himself from the atrocities. He has officially severed relations with Poland on trumped up and totally unjustified grounds. He has broken the 1941 Soviet-Poland Non-Aggression Pact."

"That's tantamount to admitting guilt." Michal mused, "The old-adage rings true. War does make strange bedfellows.

"Oh," Michal handed over the legal pad. "I have written down the figures of the victims of Katyn as monetary sums that reference the deposition of a phony legal case."

"I'm proud of your conspiratorial tactics, Michal. And you said you didn't have it in you."

Michal recalled the scene in the café and laughed. "Zygmunt, you gave me no preliminary instructions on how to conduct myself, and once I realized I had the right man, I introduced myself and called him Herr Schtingle, providing him with the role of a witness in the deposition scene of my fictitious legal brief."

Kaminski fell back in his chair laughing. "You lawyers are born conspirators; you conspire against everyone in opposition to your case."

"Oh, before you leave..." he searched about in his pockets for a small slip of paper. "Here are the call letters to a radio station in London where Zamski can be reached."

"I already have this information. You keep it, Michal, you'll be needing it." He flashed a large smile and filed out the door, leaving the attorney to ponder what else his friend held in store for him.

Michal entered his apartment later in the afternoon and found everyone actively engaged in a project of their own. Janina was in the kitchen preparing an early dinner. That was his first stop. He had worked through lunch to be home in time to eat dinner before taking the family to the cinema.

"Good evening, Janina. What are we having for dinner tonight?"

"Praise be Jesus Christ, Pan. We have fresh caught fish from the Vistula."

"Janina, you went fishing?"

She went along with the jibe. "Yes, I caught Piotrek with his basket full as he was coming home from the river."

"See that, you are learning how to shop outside the black market. Good for you."

He opened the door to Leona's office. "Almost finished Love?"

"I finished my work hours ago. I've already bathed and only need to change my clothes for my first visit to the cinema in four years."

"I take it that you are excited over the event?"

"Not excited, it's more like anxiety. I'm filled with fear, not only at the thought of attending a restricted activity, but also with the prospect of witnessing more horrors of war."

"I have those feelings as well. Will Irena be accompanying us?"

"Yes, strangely enough she doesn't seem to be suffering any angst over the situation."

There was a minimum of conversation at the table during the meal. Janina moved about the table without comment. After desert was served, Michal broke the silence.

"Janina, we'll all help clear the table and the kitchen so you can change for the cinema."

"That won't be necessary, Pan. I won't be going."

Michal looked up at her quizzically. She caught the meaning behind the look and responded.

"I have seen enough of restrictions and retributions. The bodies of innocent citizens shot in the streets for acts of violence they never committed are enough for me. I don't need to see Ruskie massacres."

Michal's voice took on a gentle tone, "I understand, Janina."

"Besides, I'm a nobody. I would never be brave enough to do anything to help during this occupation. I just want it to end." She started to cry.

Leona rose from her seat and put her arm around her. "You help yourself to a few stiff drinks of brandy before you go to bed, Janina."

The Cinema Warszawa served a full house for the showing of the film, *Soviet Massacre of Polish Officers*. The usual chatter of the crowd was absent. In its place was a somber silence as Warszawians settled into their seats prepared to witness the atrocities that the title implied.

The film was most graphic in its display of bones stacked in huge piles. The documentary panned in on the Kozelsk Prisoner of War Camp in Smolensk, Russia. This had been the former home of the victims. The scene shifted to the area in the forest where the victims were supposedly slaughtered. A mournful dirge served to underscore the horror. The narrator spoke perfect Polish. The tone and verbiage were designed to elicit an emotional response of justified anger, along with a desire for future retribution against the Stalin Regime.

The overall consensus of the after-theatre group was not the vindictive tirade the Gestapo had hoped for. The citizens of Warsaw were resolute, not reactionary. They knew of the Soviets hostility toward their political position of an independent Poland. They considered Russia as their second enemy. The prevailing reaction seemed to be, "What difference who? One enemy is just as bad as the other."

The Bednarek's lingered in the lobby; many of their friends had also come to view the film, and this was a rare occasion to mingle. Contrary to the objective coolness Irena displayed at the onset, she was visibly disturbed by what she had seen. Michal held his arm around her.

A distinguished looking gentleman, sporting a small mustache and prince nez spectacles gave a respectful smile and a slight nod of his head as he walked by them.

Michal recognized him and called out. "Professor Wiadek!"

The professor turned and seemed to appreciate the recognition. "Pan Bednarek, wonderful to see you and your lovely wife."

Michal drew Irena closer to him. "Allow me to introduce my lovely daughter, Irena."

Wiadek took her hand and kissed it. "Good evening, Irena. Your father is right; truly, you are lovely."

"Thank you, Pan. I'm happy to meet you."

Leona smiled warmly, "Professor, how fortuitous that we should meet you here."

He seemed a bit perplexed, "How so, Professor Bednarek?"

"I was planning to seek you out for an invitation to dinner one night, whenever your busy calendar will allow."

"That is indeed fortuitous for me." He reached into his vest pocket and produced a card. "Please, call on me so that we can arrive at a date. Is this invitation extended to Pani Wiadek as well?"

"Most assuredly; is she here tonight?"

"No, she chose to avoid the experience. But do call; we shall be most happy to spend an evening with good company."

Michal and he shook hands, and the professor left the crowded lobby.

"Tata, who was that?"

"Oh, that was Professor Adam Wiadek; one of the principal architects of the Prudential Building."

# CHAPTER 17

The continuous bombardment within the Ghetto walls raged on for weeks, without respite. Father Lipinski's homilies for the last month were based on the Old Testament and the Israelite's belief in one omniscient God. "The foundation of Christianity."

Just before dawn on Sunday morning, the perpetual bombardment of the ghetto ceased. It ended as abruptly as it began. Father's homily at mass that morning was a requiem for the Jews.

The mailbox on the wall of Michal's office held a newspaper wrapped in a large red label. He lifted it from the rack and felt an ominous swelling in his chest. This was Tuesday. The Polish Journal was delivered on Thursday.

He dropped his briefcase and the mail on his desk, and tore at the label that bound the issue.

SPECIAL EDITION

POLAND'S JOURNAL     May 18, 1943

GENECIDE

On April 19, 1943, the Gestapo entered the Ghetto quarter, prepared to liquidate the population of Jews remaining within the compound. It was the evening of the Old Testament commemoration of the Jewish Passover. It was Easter Monday of the Christian celebration of the

Resurrection of the Lord. The Polish flag and the Star of David waved in the breeze high above the walls of the Ghetto.

The Germans broke into the homes of the Jews and dragged them into the streets. The brutal roundup of victims had occurred many times before. The scene was repetitious in its process. Men, women, and children, were herded into lines that followed a maze of streets, encased by high walls. The inhabitants were then prodded and shoved along the final walk from their homes. Cattle cars, with the enduring stench of former victims, waited for yet another consignment of desperate people to be transported to the death house of Treblinka.

This time, however, the usual submissive resignation of the condemned was disrupted by the sound of heavy firing. Hand grenades flew from all directions. Shell fire flew from doors and windows to blast the Germans in their tracks.

S.S. reinforcements forced their way into the Ghetto, only to be fired at by machine gun fire at close range. The indomitable presence of armored vehicles was unable to withstand the onslaught. Several of them were destroyed, the others withdrew.

As invading batteries of German forces broke into the main street of the Ghetto, the walls of homes in surrounding Warsaw shook from the bombardment. When the rebels' supply of ammunition dwindled, the fighters resorted to torching the factories within the confines of the Ghetto.

The Germans adopted the tactic. They began to set fire to the homes. Tear gas and poison gas were used to route the Jews from their hiding places. Those that remained alive, were collected and funneled through the maze to Umschlag Platz. There, the noxious cattle cars awaited their victim's final journey to Treblinka.

Sporadic fighting continued. When the Jews ran out of ammunition, they resorted to rocks and clubs to pound on the Germans.

May 16, saw the end of the carnage. The compound was obliterated. The last Jew was killed.

The smoking ashes of the Ghetto stand as a tribute to a people who looked at evil and saw it for what it was. They preferred to die fighting, rather than submit to an inevitable death as sacrificial lambs.

They were our compatriots. Warsaw suffers a great and tragic loss.

# CHAPTER 18

Spring brought a large flow of shoppers to the Open Market. The warm weather was an invitation to indulge in picking through the new lettuce and early vegetables. Some made purchases, others just looked and wished, while the accomplished shop lifters hovered about waiting for a convenient moment.

A rowdy group of youngsters ran through the market, dashing around the carts.

They were members of the National Scouting Unit, the Grey Ranks. The post-war scouting organization had radically changed under the occupation. Ribbons and badges were given for valor in diversion and disruption. The younger tier, consisting of both boys and girls, were not allowed to participate in dangerous military operations. They were restricted to operations of minor sabotage and served as messengers for underground communication.

"Felix!" A thin and spindly youth approached the stand and threw his arms around him.

He wriggled out of the embrace, "Milosz, what are you playing at?"

Several of the other boys gathered around the stand and Felix could have used another pair of eyes to guard against pilferage.

"We are on a reconnaissance mission, setting up targets for this evening. We have paint and brushes…" Milosz broke off his speech when he saw the look of surprise mingled with caution in Felix' eyes.

"Yes, yes, well, I wish you luck with the canvases you will be painting for the little play you are planning."

He said aloud to the bystanders, "We have Shakespeare and his troupe, preparing for an entertainment they plan on giving at the church."

Milosz delivered a shy smile; the other boys appeared perplexed.

"That's right," Milosz acknowledged, "Come on fellows, we need to get started on our project."

He gave Felix a slap on the back and ushered his friends away from the stand and out of the market.

That evening, just before curfew, two separate groups of Grey Ranks descended on the town. One group carried cans of white paint in one hand, a fine bristled brush in the other. They scattered about the area, randomly applying the paint to easily visible structures. Some crude, and some artistic, versions of the "anchor" the logo for the slogan, "Fighting Poland," were embellished on walls and over Nazi placards around the business district of City Center.

The other group was armed with screwdrivers and hammers, to remove the new German street signs, and replace them with the original Polish names.

Felix saw the brazen disruption from his truck as he pulled out of the market. He pulled over and parked his truck between two buildings and ran up to a group of boys who were changing the street signs on the corner.

"Idiots, do you know what you are doing?"

The projects were in full swing when the authorities burst upon the scene. Screeching cars and blaring sirens filled the street with Gendarme and Blue Police. Shots rang out dispersing citizens still on the streets before curfew. The uniformed men, shooting randomly into the fleeing pedestrians, turned the neighborhood into a war zone.

Milosz was stretching from the bannister of a balcony. Deftly holding onto a paint brush, he attempted to put the flourishing touch to the elegant rope that wound its way around his anchor. Bullets flew by him, but there was still that extra stroke that would make his anchor a work of art. One of the bullets made its mark in the center of his back. He lurched forward, tottering on the bannister; paint can, and brush tumbled toward the ground. Milosz clutched at his chest; a dissonant scream followed him onto the street below.

Eight boys were shot, six killed instantly, two severely wounded. Four others were herded off by the Gendarme, to Szucha Street. Milosz was among the dead, his body to be claimed by his family; if they dared.

Felix, rushed toward Milosz' body in the street. A gendarme took direct aim at Felix' head. The bullet found its mark in his right temple.

Virski of Civil Resistance received the report of the unauthorized Boy Scout disruption. He immediately notified Dysthmus.

# CHAPTER 19

The dark green Opel Kapitan slowly approached the Duzat drive. Dysthmus was rehearsing the proper phrasing he would use to announce the sudden death of a young and vibrant young man.

He was most concerned with how Ludwiga would handle the news. She gave the impression of indifference to the world around her. God had been good to her, neither of her sons had suffered from the war. The General Government allowed them relative safety, as long as the quota assigned them for their farm produce was maintained.

Ludwiga was the one to swing the screen door open on the porch.

"*Dobry weiczor*, Marek. You come late—Felix is not yet home. I don't know what's keeping him," receiving no answer, she went on.

"What are you doing here, after curfew?"

Dysthmus' frozen facial features and stone-like posture revealed it all. Ludwiga started to crumble. He reached forward to prevent her collapsing; somehow she managed to right herself. He wrapped his arms around her and huddled her close.

The rest of the family rushed from the porch. Dysthmus never uttered a word.

At five o'clock in the morning, Dysthmus was sitting in Felix' truck. There was an eerie silence offset only by the occasional call of a duck in the square trying to wake the flock. The city was in a state of peaceful unrest. The gendarme hadn't completed their clean-up operations from the carnage of the night before. Dysthmus tried to lift Felix' body onto the truck, but the stiff, uncompliant corpse was too heavy to manage alone. He waited for the sanitary department to make their rounds.

By now, Warsaw was a city of insurgents. The slogan, "Independence or Death" became a cultural icon. Collaborators were dealt with in the Secret Court as soon as they were validly identified. All Poles could be counted on to aid in the underground in whatever manner they could.

The dull grinding sound of the street cleaner approached the corner. Dysthmus climbed out of the truck and waited for the crew to drive by; he flagged them down.

"Men, I could use some help with my friend's body over there. The family is anxious to give him a decent burial." He made the sign of the cross with a rosary.

"Quickly," the driver rasped.

Two other men jumped out of the truck.

Dysthmus turned to run, "I'll pull my truck up!"

The transfer occurred in a matter of minutes, and Dysthmus was on his way to take Felix home.

Kaminski attended the funeral. He pulled Dysthmus aside, "What about the other boy, the scout?"

Dysthmus offered what little he knew of the boy. "The family lives under the direst conditions. His father was a carpenter, and able to provide the basic necessities, but he was killed in a roundup. Milosz' body was burned, along with the others that were left in the streets after the anchor disturbance."

The Majek family lived in a basement apartment; a sub-standard facility without heat or running water. Kaminski made his way through littered trash, some in bags others strewn about, food for the vermin. He braved the stench and knocked on the basement door. There was no answer, but he could hear scuffling and movement going on inside.

"Please, Pani, I am from Civil Resistance, and I want to know if we can be of some help."

The sound of a key released the lock and the knob turned, revealing a slight, very thin woman, possibly in her sixties—war ravaged the body internally and externally, she may have been younger. She looked up at Kaminski.

"May I step inside?"

She moved out of his path, allowing him admittance. There were two small children huddled by a make shift fire-pit built of cinder block with a grill on top. Something was cooking in a large metal pot. The smell was rather pleasant.

"What's that you're cooking?"

"Nettle soup. My sister picked some yesterday. They're still young and fresh."

"Are these your children?"

The two little ones sat on the floor staring up at him with an anxious look in their eyes.

"No, they are my sister's. She sews uniforms for the Germans." She gathered her shawl tightly about her and moved closer to the stove.

"It's just you and your sister?"

"No, her husband, he works on the trash trucks."

"How do you manage without water?"

"The neighbor on the third floor let us use her toilet and gives us water for cooking and washing."

"So, you share your ration cards with your sister and brother-in-law?"

"Yes, but we still starve. Manya, my sister brings home machine oil, when she can slip it in her pail. Edmund brings home whatever he can find from collecting. He is good for bringing wood and paper for the fire."

"What's the machine oil for?"

"We use it to fry orache and bran cakes. When nettle is fresh, we make soup and tea."

Kaminski was familiar with the ingredients. The plants were seasonal and could be found in nearby vacant lots. Nettles in the spring and orache in the fall.

"Where do you get the bran?"

"My brother-in-law collects it from the mills. They sift it out when they grind the wheat."

Kaminski dug into his pocket, "Pani, use this for whatever you need most, but I offer it for some warm clothing for the children."

Her eyes flooded with tears. She grabbed his hands and kissed them.

He gently touched her shoulder and lowered his voice, "I will make a report to Civil Resistance. They will be able to help."

He could not bring himself to mention Milosz.

# CHAPTER 20

Edward Potopski turned the key to the padlock and removed it from its bracket on the door. He picked up the parcels that were lying just outside the threshold and stepped inside to begin another day as manager of the shop he once owned.

Herr Gruffman, a wealthy Schindlerite, bought the property as an investment and had Potopski stay on to manage the shop. During negotiations for the sale, he was assured by the Gestapo that Potopski was a collaborator who had proved his ability to inform on persons of interest and could be trusted.

Potopski had only one reason to stay alive. He was dedicated to the eventual destruction of the occupiers. He worked in conjunction with the Civil Resistance. The Stationery Store became a refuge for traveling insurgents and offered a secure hideout for covert meetings.

Kaminski supplied the merchandise that filled the shelves. On his most recent visit, he nodded a greeting to Edward and went directly to the basement.

Virski, a high-ranking officer in Civil Resistance, sat drumming his fingers on the table. A man of average height and muscular physique, he appeared to be in his forties. He had no distinguishing facial features, his hair was light and thinning. In fact, there was a vague ordinary quality about him that made it difficult to describe; no doubt this contributed to his continued success in the field of espionage.

Kaminski dragged a stool to the table. "We have the cooperation of Niegorski, Chief of Paviak Police."

Virski narrowed his eyes. Niegorski was the chief of police of Warsaw's peacetime Blue Police. The Nazis took over the command and continued to utilize the force to keep law and order of the city's inhabitants and those who were incarcerated in the prisons.

"Somehow or other, Niegorski has been able to walk a very tight rope. He maintains control over that traitorous force of his, while he continues to be available to us whenever we need him."

Virski shrugged his shoulders.

Kaminski went on. "Well, we need him now. I have worked it out with Niegorski. Tavish is to feign a stroke."

"Will the old man be able to pull it off?"

"Yes, it's just a matter of slobbering and gibbering while he feigns an inability to use his right arm. He can do it. It will seem a serious condition that must be treated at the hospital, as it is not easily diagnosed. So far, he has divulged nothing of consequence to his torturers, so they still hold an interest in him."

"Who's in charge of the transport?"

"If it's alright with you, Dysthmus; unless you have someone else in mind."

"Dysthmus is perfect. I think he is in league with the devil; he never gets caught."

"He has already laid the ground work. He delivers medical supplies to the infirmary, and he's made friends with the staff by plying them with presents of vodka and sausage."

"The timing is crucial."

"That's where Dysthmus' devil comes in to play. We have everything coordinated down to the last minute, but there's always that unaccountable hitch to a situation that can crop up and throw everything out the window."

"It's worth the try. Where will you take the old man?"

"To a monastery, a few miles outside of Warsaw. I have spoken with the prelate who is only too pleased to accommodate Tavish. This is a matter of complete secrecy."

Virski interjected, "I can't overemphasize the need for secrecy. Somewhere, within the underground is a spy. As yet, we have no idea who it might be, so we are all the more cautious in our operations. We have lost six valuable officers who were either murdered or imprisoned in the last few months. Someone, either in the Home Army or Civil Resistance is passing information along to the Gestapo."

Kaminski had already been apprised of the situation. He was holding it on the back burner, until there was a solution.

"The only ones to be aware of this rescue mission are the principal players; Niegorski, Dysthmus, you, myself, and of course, Tavish."

"When is this to take place?"

"This Wednesday at noon; it's payday for the staff, and at lunch there will be only one nurse on duty. Most of the staff will be focused on how they'll be spending their money. If the pieces fit together, without a disruption, we'll have him home safe."

# CHAPTER 21

Dysthmus whistled a sprightly tune as he walked the hall to the infirmary. He carried a huge box labeled '*Arznei*,' German for medicine. He juggled the box as he tried to open the door. Franz, the corpsman on duty, heard the whistling and rushed to greet him.

"Ah, Dielinski, it's you." His attention was on the box. "So, you bring us medicine?"

Dysthmus responded to the name that was inscribed on his current driver's license and work permit.

"Yes, happy medicine." He pulled out two bottles of vodka and a large package that contained five pounds of assorted sausages.

Franz quickly took one of the bottles and hid it under the cot that held his one and only patient.

"What's wrong with the old codger?"

Tavish did not react. He kept his eyes on the ceiling above.

"Stroke." Franz pulled a brown paper bag from a drawer in the desk and proceeded to extricate the sausage for his share of the contraband treasure.

"What's going to be done for him?"

"I don't know; the doctor is at the hospital." He replied in an off-handed manner.

Niegorski walked in on them; allowing the weight of his stature and uniform to fill the room with a sense of authority. "What's this smell—meat?"

Franz shuffled the bag onto the table where the delicacy sat throwing off its aroma of meat and garlic. "It's a special treat for the staff from Pan Dielinski."

Niegorski plucked up the bottle of vodka. "And this?"

Dysthmus interrupted. "Listen Officer, you have an old man over here that is in dire need of immediate medical attention. Unless you have no concern for his life, I think he is more important than the vodka."

Franz gave a sigh of relief and the color returned to his face.

Niegorski looked over to the cot. Saliva was pooling around the old man's chin.

"That's Ignatz Tavish. What is being done for him?"

"We are waiting for the doctor." Franz blurted.

"How long have you been waiting?"

"He came in here a half hour ago."

"And where is the doctor?"

"At the hospital."

Niegorski shot over to the desk and picked up the phone. "General Greiner…this is urgent." A long pause, during which time Franz' breathe quickened, and Niegorski twisted the phone wire in his hand.

"General… Officer Niegorski here, we have Tavish in the infirmary, obviously with a stroke… he's at the hospital…very well."

He placed the phone in the cradle and lifted it up again, "Ambulance to the infirmary, immediately."

He walked over to the cot. "How are you, Tavish?"

Tavish continued to stare up at the ceiling.

Time hovered over the scene, while the three men waited for the appearance of the paramedics. Finally, the driver of an ambulance entered the infirmary lugging a collapsible gurney.

"Where's your partner?" Niegorski demanded.

"He is suffering with dysentery, Sir."

Niegorski was about to react, when Dysthmus intervened.

"We need to get him into the ambulance. I'll help." He pulled the gurney from the driver; both men tugged at Tavish and put him onto the stretcher. Franz handed the patient file to the driver and the old man was wheeled to the elevator.

Niegorski stayed behind to fill out his duty report and write up an order of reprimand for the attending corpsman.

The cobblestone courtyard was deserted. Payday at lunch hour was a busy time for the gendarme and staff. Dysthmus and the driver rushed the gurney over the rough surface of the yard to the waiting ambulance; their patient bounced about on the stretcher. The driver let go of his end and turned to open the ambulance door. Dysthmus drew the hammer from his pocket and delivered a swift blow that landed directly on the center of the driver's head. He dropped down to his knees and then he fell to the ground.

Dysthmus turned to observe the approaching figure of Kaminski.

"Good Shot!" He grabbed the hammer from Dysthmus and shoved it in his pocket, he whispered, "So far, so good."

A black Mercedes pulled up behind them, Virski came out from behind the wheel. Kaminski and Dysthmus helped the old man into the back seat of the Mercedes. Kaminski took the wheel with Virski seated next to him. The Mercedes took off and Dysthmus picked up a rock to inflict a wound to his forehead; he positioned himself over the collapsed gurney. The driver began to move about on the ground. Dysthmus yelled out. "Help! Help!"

Workers from the nearby buildings rushed over to the scene. Dysthmus stumbled over to aid the driver. He shouted, "We've been attacked. Someone has kidnapped a patient." He looked down at the driver, "Are you alright?"

# CHAPTER 22

Niegorski was summoned to the office of the commanding general of Paviak Prison.

The corpsman, Franz Koeppel, was seated on a bench outside General Greiner's office. A gendarme stood on either side of the door. Koeppel stood at attention when Niegorski approached. The guards saluted the chief of police, and he returned the gesture.

He entered the office and found the general seated at his desk; his secretary was seated next to him with pad and pencil, ready to record the proceedings of an impromptu trial. Another guard was posted inside the door. Off in a corner, Doctor Menning, the prison's physician, sat with his coat on and his hat in his lap.

Niegorski saluted the general and stood at attention.

"Officer Niegorski, we are here to determine exactly what occurred in the infirmary with prisoner Tavish. Please, be seated."

Niegorski took a seat. The general continued.

"I have your report on the incident as it occurred up until the abduction. I also have your order of reprimand for the orderly Franz Koeppel." He adjusted the documents on his desk. "We have not yet received the report on the alarm you sent after the prisoner was abducted. Begin with what led to the alarm."

Niegorski started to stand. "Remain seated officer, this is an informal hearing. Go on."

"I had my reports in my hand and was on my way to your office to deliver them, when I accosted Pan Dielinski, the delivery man, rushing up the stairs. His head was bleeding and he seemed very upset. He said that he and the driver of the ambulance were attacked and rendered unconscious by blows to the head. Dielinski stated that when he regained his senses, the prisoner, who was about to be transported to the hospital, had disappeared. That was when I sent in the alarm. I have not had time to write up a report."

"What did the delivery man have to say about the abductors?"

"He never saw them. The ambulance driver was still groggy from his blow and was unable to provide any details."

"We have already spoken with the orderly, who has no information at all on the abduction." He motioned to the guard. "Have the delivery man brought in."

Niegorski's interest peaked. How would Dysthmus handle himself? He felt confident that he would pull it off.

Dysthmus was led into the room by the guard; he walked over to the General's desk, cap in hand; ready for questioning.

"Your name?"

"Dielinski, Viktor."

"Your position?"

"Independent distributor."

"You are not employed?"

"My truck and I are under contract to the Schultz Sewing Machine Factory, which is currently manufacturing weapons. I am at their beck and call, but since there are few reliable delivery men about town, I take on side jobs whenever my services are not required by Schultz."

He stressed the word 'reliable' hoping that it would be construed as "collaborator."

"And what occurred early this afternoon in the infirmary?"

"I made a delivery to the infirmary and noticed an old man lying on the cot. He made no movement and I thought he was dead. I asked the orderly about him and was told that he had suffered a stroke. At that moment, Officer Niegorski entered the room and seemed upset that the prisoner was not attended to by the doctor who was at the hospital. He made a call to you and then he called for an ambulance. The driver answered the call, but he was by himself. He said his partner was suffering from diarrhea, so I offered to help transport the prisoner to the ambulance. Once outside, someone struck the driver from behind. I turned to look and was hit in the head. When I came to I found the driver lying on the ground; the gurney was turned over and empty. I tried to help the driver and then I ran into the building to alert Officer Niegorski."

The General raised his eyebrows and looked directly at Dysthmus. "This is a vitally important issue; one that will have serious repercussions. Pan Dielinski, due to the urgency of the matter, I'm afraid we must detain you until this investigation is completed. We will need your contact number at the factory. Please leave the necessary information with my secretary."

He motioned to the guard, "Take Pan Dielinski to the warden, along with this notice." He scribbled something on a piece of paper and handed it to the guard. "I hope you find the accommodations suitable for a reliable delivery man, Pan Dielinski."

# CHAPTER 23

Dysthmus was led from the administration offices of Paviak Prison by an armed guard. They walked through the courtyard where the scene of abduction had occurred a mere two hours before.

The bright afternoon sun did little to offset the gloom of the pervading gray of the buildings and the haunting specter of hordes of former prisoners who had previously made this trip to their incarceration.

Two guards stood sentry duty at opposite sides of the entrance to the prison proper. They moved to open the massive doors for the approaching prisoner. The guard that made the trek with Dysthmus, raised his right arm and clicked his heels, "Hiel Hitler." His salute was immediately returned along with resounding clicks and "Hiels."

They entered a cavernous dark hall and were greeted by a noxious odor that caused Dysthmus to gasp. He took short breaths in an effort to control the effect of the stench. The guard proceeded through the hall, seemingly unaffected by the smell.

The cells along the walls were filled to capacity and additional mattresses were strewn on the floor to accommodate the overflow. The extensive lavatory was latrine fashioned with a huge hose attached to a massive plug in the wall to wash away the feces and urine.

The guard stopped beyond the lavatory and assigned his prisoner a spot along the wall.

"You will billet here, on this mattress. You have access to the table in the corner for your meals or for writing purposes."

"Is the General aware that I have no toiletries for bathing, or a change of clothes?"

"I have been given no directive on this issue. That is something you will have to work out for yourself."

He turned and made his way back down the passage through the huge hall. Dysthmus stared after him, a look of disbelief on his face.

"This is not a place you will grow used to, my friend."

An elderly man with a scraggly beard and an unkempt appearance addressed him from a mattress on the floor.

Dysthmus bent down to get a good look at the man. "Have you been here long?"

"Long enough to indulge in fantasies of my bath and shower at home and the good meals I took for granted."

Dysthmus looked about him on the floor for a space to sit; he decided to remain standing.

"Why are you here?"

"I suspect that some Nazi officer, or other, has decided he would like to take up residence in my domicile." He extended his hand up to Marek. "Allow me to introduce myself; I am Count Zarzitski, from Mokotow."

The Count's predicament seemed valid, and if it was true, he would never be released to reclaim his estate.

"I'm truly sorry for you, old man."

He looked around again at the overcrowded conditions of the hall.

"Don't they ever move these prisoners on to another place?"

"Yes, but something of vital importance must be going on, because they just recently filled this hall with victims."

Dysthmus braved the lavatory in search of some towels. Lying in a corner were some rags that were available for an eventual necessity. He gathered up a few and lathered them with the strong lye soap that was sitting on a sink. He found a corner near his assigned billet, situated under a barred window, and scrubbed away a spot for himself.

He had been relieved of his watch by the gendarme who accompanied him to the prison and there was no clock within the confines of the hall. He judged by the light in the window that it was going on to dusk. A clatter of wheels and clinking of metal approached from the opposite direction of the entrance. Two Blue Police were wheeling a cart with a huge kettle. On a shelf, to the side of the cart, were rows of bowls. Dinner was being served.

One policeman poured a liquid into the bowls as the other man stood by with a club in his hand; he appeared ready to use it.

The men rushed at the cart and scrambled to get a bowl of the liquid. The armed man pulled a pistol from his holster and shot a bullet at the ceiling. "Wait your turn or meet your maker." The scuffle subsided for a bit, only to gain momentum as the slimy liquid appeared to be reaching the bottom of the pot.

Dysthmus was not interested in obtaining a bowl of the putrefied soup. He had recognized the server as a school chum with whom he had shared many a boyhood misadventure.

He waited until he heard the metal scooper scrape against the bottom of the pot. The armed guard was trying to maintain order. Dysthmus sidled over to the cart.

"Walek, so this is how you wound up; on the other side of the law?"

The officer searched the face of the prisoner and recognized a former classmate. "Marek, were you dragged in as a hostage?"

"No, I'm here under an unlawful lock-up. I'm an innocent victim."

"Almost everyone here is a victim."

"What are you talking about, 'hostages'?"

"Governor Frank is in Warsaw on a short visit. He's staying at what used to be the Czech Ambassador's place on Chopin Street."

"What's that got to do with hostages?"

"In the event any disturbance occurs while Frank is in Warsaw, these men will be shot before a firing squad. There's fifty-six of them, most of them former elite of Warsaw."

"Does that include the Count over there?"

"Yes, we have honored guests that include artists, musicians, and political figures." He tittered, "I am rubbing elbows with the rich and famous, who are now non-entities and poor."

Dysthmus smirked. "Well, maybe they'll let the old Count go after Frank leaves town."

Early the next morning, the prisoners were growling and becoming a rowdy bunch. Whatever the gruel was that they received the night before hadn't sustained them; they were eager for breakfast. Marek had no interest in food; freedom was on his mind.

The anticipated breakfast carts had not yet appeared, when two guards entered the area.

"Victor Dielinski?"

Dysthmus raised his hand. "Here!"

"Come with us."

The return walk through the dark hall seemed less repugnant than the odious trek the day before. He was marched out the door and back to the familiar administration building.

The guards accompanied him into the elevator and one of them pulled the handle to start the car upward. When they reached the fourth floor, the guard brought the handle to a stop, slid the expandable gate back on its hinges and pulled the metal door open to exit the car.

Dysthmus knew exactly where he was. He was being led to General Griever's Office.

The same complement of guards stood duty; only this time the faces were different. The secretary was again seated on the general's left; he appeared to be busy studying a document.

One of the accompanying guards addressed the General. "Hiel Hitler!" his heels clicked, "Here is the prisoner, Dielinski."

Greiner was examining a document on his desk. The response was slow to come. "Ah yes, the distributor of the Schultz Sewing Machine Company."

Dysthmus swallowed hard. His only hope was that his friend, Joseph, a reliable partisan, had been the one to answer the phone.

"The office manager has confirmed your position with the firm. He also registered a complaint and admitted to some urgency for your immediate deployment to the shop. It seems orders are waiting for delivery."

He finally looked up at Dysthmus. "I hope your stay with us was a memorable one and that you will do your best not to return."

He scratched his name onto a form and handed it to the guard. "Escort this man to his vehicle which has been impounded in the garage. Here is an order for its release."

Dysthmus clicked his heels, "Thank you General!"

There was no response.

# CHAPTER 24

The parish housekeeper, Pani Trypka, led Leona to the study where Father Lipinski sat reading his Breviary.

"Ah, Leona; how are you my dear?"

"Fine, Father. Am I interrupting your prayers?"

"Yes, but the good Lord and I will overlook the disruption." He laid the book down on the table and stood to welcome her. "Is this a social call, or shall I get my purple stole for a confession?"

She smiled warmly as she took the hand he offered her. "Actually, it has to do with a social invitation."

"Please, take a seat. Do you have time for some sherry?"

"Thank you, no Father. I'm on my way to class. We are having some friends over to dinner this Saturday evening, and we'd like to have you join us. I hope this doesn't come as short notice, but the date fits the busy schedules of both Michal and Dr. Wiadek, our other invited guest. I'm sure the conversation will be most interesting, and I look forward to your contribution to the evening."

"Well, that means I will have to speed up work on my homily for Sunday, but yes, I shall be most happy to attend. I look forward to Janina's good cooking and stimulating conversation with good friends. What time shall I be there?"

"Is five o'clock too early? We'd like the dinner to be leisurely. There's the curfew to consider."

"Very well, the timing is good for me. What shall I bring?"

"Your blessings."

Just before noon on Friday, two men dressed in the brown shirts and gray uniforms of the Gestapo were ushered into the parish office by Pani Trypka. Her voice trembled as she asked them to wait while she went to summon Father.

Lipinski was in the garden when the official Gestapo car pulled up to the parish house. He smiled warmly at his housekeeper when she came running to fetch him.

He nodded his head, "I know Magda; I'm coming."

His response did nothing to alleviate the look of fear on her face.

"It's alright, Magda, God is in his heaven, and all is right in the world." He walked ahead of her into the house.

The two men were standing at attention when he entered the office. "Please, Gentlemen, have a seat."

The Sergeant responded with the usual straight arm salute, "Hiel Hitler, we are here to escort you to an audience with Governor General Frank."

Lipinski had heard the rumors that Frank had traveled from his headquarters in Cracow to be smuggled into the home of the former Czech Legation for a visit with the Governor of Warsaw, Ludwig Fischer. He was not about to feign ignorance of the matter.

"One moment; I'll just get my hat and tell my housekeeper that I shall not be here for lunch."

The higher-ranking member of the two, the sergeant, acknowledged the request,

"Schnell!"

On the walk to the auto, Lipinski appeared taller than his escorts. He marched between the Gestapo men in his usual slow and measured stride. When the officers goaded him to walk faster, he offered a benign smile and nodded his head, but continued at his natural pace.

The car made a turn onto Chopin Street and swung up the long road that led to a building at the far end, which now housed the administrative offices of the General Government of Warsaw. The driver wheeled the vehicle into a slot in front of the door. A sign attached to a pole on the curb marked the spot as VERBOTTEN in large red letters. The driver remained in his seat as the sergeant got out and opened the back door for the priest. They entered the building and Lipinski was led through a queue of offices where clerks and officials sat working at their desks. The end of the hall opened into a lavishly appointed apartment.

Governor General Hans Frank was comfortably ensconced in an overstuffed chair, his drink sat next to him on a small end table, and he held a cigar in his hand. Seated across from him, appearing every bit as comfortable was the Governor of Warsaw, SA-Gruppenfuhrer Ludwig Fischer, Dr. of Jurisprudence. There was a commonality about the two men; both were solidly built, with broad faces and strong features. Their physical appearance suggested men who were in command of themselves and their surroundings; men who were not only resolute, but immutable.

The sergeant delivered his "Hiel" and a click of his heels. "Governor Frank, Father Jan Lipinski."

Both men remained seated. Fischer responded. "Thank you, Sergeant." The officer saluted once more and left the room. Lipinski moved forward.

"Good afternoon, Father. Won't you join us in a drink?" Frank offered.

"Good afternoon, sherry if you please."

"Off course, please be seated." He pointed to the seat on the other side of the small table that held his glass of whiskey.

Lipinski nodded a greeting to Fischer and settled in the chair, while Frank ordered a sherry from the server.

Frank picked up the conversation. "We are expecting you to join us for lunch. I hope you have brought an appetite."

"As a matter of fact, I have as yet to break bread for the day. There are two masses to serve on Friday. I shall be most happy to join you."

"How are your parishioners fairing, Father?"

Lipinski had no tolerance for hypocrisy. He caught his breath and cocked his head to the side. "In what way do you mean, Governor?"

Before he could answer, the server returned to announce that lunch was being served, "Father's sherry is at his place at table."

Frank asked the priest to say grace; the two German's joined in for the blessing.

The conversation began on a mundane note. The balmy May weather, the possibility of continued good weather for crops, the attendance at church, and then the Governor General introduced the subject that Lipinski sat in fear of addressing.

"We have been trying to have a meeting with the Cardinal in Cracow for the last two years. We have yet to receive a plausible excuse for his ignoring our invitations."

The priest looked directly into Frank's eyes. "Since the war, His Eminence is not as accessible as he was at one time. Matters of the church have become compounded during the unrest. Many of the religious community have lost their lives or been imprisoned, and there is no way of replacing the loss with new novitiates. The German government has closed all schools of higher learning, including the seminaries. Also, because of the suffering of Polish citizens, the Cardinal has become more contemplative. And there is always the fear of breaching the cardinal rule of the New Testament, "Render to Caesar the things that are Caesar's and to God the things that are God's." He left off with a benign smile.

"Very eloquently put, Father. I should enjoy sitting in your church to hear one of your homilies, but I too have my restrictions due to the war." He raised his glass to toast the priest.

The servers came to clear away the dishes of the main course and conversation stalled. Once coffee was served, Fischer, Governor of Warsaw, introduced a new tact.

"I have informed the Governor General that Warsaw has been holding its own in revenue provided to the Reich. The taxes collected in recent years have equaled or gone beyond those of Cracow, Radom, and Lublin. The Governor General has given this issue some consideration."

Lipinski prepared himself for some bewildering propaganda to emerge from this outlandish assessment. How could this be possible? Resistance had become a way of life among Warszawians. Where was all this complicity coming from?

Frank took up the obvious "pitch." "The Reich is giving serious consideration of offering concessions to the Polish people. We are considering the increase of food supplies and re-establishing the secondary education of the nation, along with wider employment opportunities within the administration."

Lipinski did not exhibit by gesture or facial expression any response to the carrots Frank had waved in front of him.

There was a note of disdain in the Governor's concluding comment.

"Perhaps these new concessions will enable the Cardinal to spend less time in contemplation and more time in cooperation."

"Governor Frank, the easing of these restrictions will most certainly raise the living standards of our people, and we shall look forward to the inception of these conditions. As always, we shall be grateful to God, who is the ultimate purveyor of good."

# CHAPTER 25

Kaminski dropped by the office with a plate of *pierogi* from the Chestnut Café and a bottle of black-market champagne. Michal was agog, "What's this?"

"Tavish is free and safely sequestered!" He announced.

Leona was in the dining room arranging the seating order; she was stressed and cranky; it was years since she hosted this large a party. Before the war, professional associates of academia, the political scene, and the legal system shared meals and engaged in stimulating conversations at the Bednarek table on a regular basis. The elite were in hiding and there was a severe food shortage. Tonight's guests held legitimate *Ausbeis* cards and Leona stretched the larder budget to shop the black market. Getting the apartment up to the standards that would satisfy her was no longer in the hands of a maid; she and Irena ran the vacuum and wielded the feather duster and polish to undergo the anticipated scrutiny of the guests. Janina had been in the kitchen before breakfast preparing culinary dishes from the past, with an ample supply of vegetables from the Open Market, contraband vodka and other items available only from the black market. The visit of the esteemed Wiadeks was causing quite a bustle.

Michal entered the scene smiling and amiable; he gave the traditional greeting, "Praise be Jesus Christ."

From the living room, Irena called out, "Forever and ever."

Leona stood still and waited for her husband to approach; he seemed unusually jovial.

"Where have you been?"

He didn't miss the sharpness of her tone. He mustered up his courage and turned on the charm, "I have been constructively employed." He tried to kiss her cheek, but she motioned him away.

She turned her head and wrinkled her nose, "You've been drinking!"

"Kaminski stopped by..."

"It seems to me, Michal, that Zygmunt has become more important to you than your family."

He took hold of her shoulders and lowered his voice a notch, "Tavish has been rescued."

She weakened under his hold and blessed herself, "Oh my God!" She reached for a chair, he helped to settle her in.

"I've invited Kaminski to dinner. Will that be alright?"

"Of course, Michal. Will he give us details this evening?"

"I can't say, but let's see what he does have to offer in the way of current events."

Rihard was the first to arrive. He perched on the edge of a chair in the living room while he waited for Irena to finish dressing. He remained perfectly still, not daring to taste the assorted canapés that Janina had set out for appetizers and aperitif. A soft Nocturne played softly on the gramophone; the stage was set.

At precisely five o'clock, the Wiadeks made their appearance at the door. A bottle of elderberry wine and a bouquet of fresh flowers was presented to Leona when she opened the door.

"Professor Bednarek, you remember my wife, Genowefa?"

Mrs. Wiadek was a tall and angular shaped woman with a warm and pleasant manner that stood in contrast to her gaunt appearance.

"Of course, I do. So pleasant to see you again, Genowefa."

Irena came into the foyer and greeted the couple, "May I have your wraps? Janina is busily engaged in performing gourmet art in the Kitchen."

Wiadek lifted his head to sniff the air. "The aroma serves to advertise her production."

Leona ushered the couple into the living room and introduced them to Rihard who stumbled out of his seat gesturing clumsily, unable to decide if he should shake the professor's hand first or go for a kiss to his wife's hand. His effort was graciously acknowledged by the pair, and he did neither.

Michal was in the middle of pouring the sherry when another rap was heard on the door. Father Lipinski and Kaminski arrived together with chocolates from one and cherry brandy from the other.

After introductions, the guests engaged in the preliminary mundane comments that occur during the "getting to know what you're about process."

Adam Wiadek initiated the serious conversation that held all of their interest.

"The German papers are filled with the news of Ignatz Tavish's abduction from Pawiak Prison at the cost of eighty innocent Poles."

Zygmunt sat deep inside his chair, his hands folded over his chest, "One hundred prisoners are hanging from the walls of the prison as a notice to passersby of the type of reprisal one can expect for rescuing prisoners." He reached for his drink, "Yes, we don't ever accomplish anything of value without having the Nazis extract something of greater value from us."

A long silence elapsed.

Leona spoke first, "Zygmunt, how did the rescue take place and where is Tavish now?"

"My dear Leona, I hope that information is never divulged, because it would mean the end of Tavish and the lives of those involved; most of whom are totally innocent."

"Thank God, he didn't wind up like Pieklakiewicz." Wiadek's comment was delivered slowly in a tone of reverence.

"Indeed. But the old, gentle professor never divulged any information to the Gestapo during his internment." Kaminski reached for a cracker and spread a dab of cheese on it, while he validated his statement. "I have an informer planted in Szucha Street. He's one of the janitors; an elderly man without family, who is willing to risk his life. He was there to witness the daily frustration of the interrogators, who got nowhere with the old gent."

Leona's seating arrangement at table afforded Rihard a seat opposite the professor.

In the interval between courses, Genowefa addressed her hostess. "Adam tells me that the invitation to dinner was given at the cinema, after the Katyn film."

"Yes, you were unable to attend?"

"I could not. My brother, a Colonel in the Polish Army, may very well have been taken prisoner at Smolensk. We have never heard from him since the invasion."

"Oh, Pani, I know how you must feel. I was very upset by the film." Irena empathized.

Leona searched for something to offer in the way of consolation, "I'm so sorry for you. You were wise not to attend."

Father Jan folded his hands and lowered his head; the others followed his cue.

"Dear Lord, we offer this prayer for all the victims of Katyn and all of the innocent souls who have been martyred during this seizure we are forced to endure."

Rihard made several attempts to engage the professor in conversation, but his efforts were so trite and naïve, that the few responses he did receive were mostly "yes" and "no."

It wasn't until brandy and coffee was served that Father Lipinski was able to report on his recent luncheon with Governor General Frank and Gruppenfuhrer Fischer, the Governor of Warsaw.

"I'm not sure it's general knowledge, but Governor General Frank is visiting Warsaw at the former Czech Embassy. Since I was invited to lunch with him, it may not be top-secret."

Kaminski gently goaded, "And you, a priest, were invited to lunch?"

"Yes, I was taken, under guard, to Chopin Street to dine with Frank and Fischer. I suspected the invitation was extended to me so that I could answer for the Cardinal, who has been avoiding Frank for four years, but there was another item on the agenda. Governor Fischer informed me that the General Government was considering a new directive for the citizens of Warsaw."

"Oh, my God, things can't get worse!"

"On the contrary, my dear Leona, and this I regard as malicious propaganda, he proposed a series of concessions. He suggested that these concessions were made because the revenue collected from Warsaw, during the last three years, far out-weighed that of Cracow, Lublin, and Radom combined."

Michal's legal mind required the facts. "What are these concessions to be?"

"An increase in food supplies, the re-establishment of secondary education, the restoration of Polish property rights, and wider opportunities for employment in the German administration."

"The directive is handed down from Goebbels." Kaminski seemed to have full knowledge of the situation.

"But is it true? Where is all this revenue coming from?"

"Yes, Father, it's true. The Schindlerites are growing fat from their enterprises. Am I not correct, Michal?"

"Quite true, they are heavily taxed on those confiscated businesses that fell to them so cheaply."

"And the black-market vodka is getting an inflated price in Berlin, where they can't get enough of the stuff."

"And what about the concessions, is that a possibility"

"They are bending at the wheel. The Allies are preparing to open a second front, somewhere in the back yard of the Reich. The Soviets frigid winter finally ousted them from Stalingrad and Smolensk, and they are unable to deliver adequate supplies to the Wehrmacht in territories they still hold. The future bodes the demise of the Third Reich."

"Then why are they considering these concessions to Warsaw?"

Kaminski snickered, "They can't make the Poles love them. The underground resistance is overwhelming them. The destruction and disruption to their military occupation is constant and they have no tangible strategies to stop these activities."

Michal offered refills of vodka and Kaminski pushed his glass forward.

"This goes back to last year. Philosophically, there is a vast difference between Himmler and Goebbels. Himmler is a throwback to the Neanderthal, he's a brute. Goebbels, though every bit as ruthless, is more of a student of human nature. He advocates that the heavy restrictions and violent punitive measures imposed on Poland helped create the vicious insurgency of the underground. He viewed his superior's governing style as a matter of "…slaughtering the cow, which they wanted to milk.""

Dr. Wiadek was impressed with the clarity of Kaminski's information. "So, Frank is taking his cue from Goebbels and Fischer will follow the edict."

"Perhaps, but don't look for this to happen in the immediate future. They are sure to take a slow and steady tact so as to sway the population into a more moderate stance. They don't want to overwhelm us with kindness and encourage suspicion as to their extreme reversal of edicts and restrictions."

Leona motioned to Janina to serve the desert. During the renewed interest in the pleasure of sweet treats, she whispered something to Irena, who immediately rose from her chair.

"Excuse me please." She looked over at Rihard and motioned him to follow her.

When Wiadek finished his cake, Leona asked that he join her in the living room.

Rihard and Irena took up seats on the settee, leaving the occasional chairs unoccupied.

"Won't you please be seated, Adam?" Leona pointed to a chair and then sat in the one facing him. She beamed a smile at him; he responded with a quizzical arching of his eyebrows.

"Please forgive me, Adam, I maneuvered you away, so that we might have a private conversation of our own."

"What is it, Leona?"

"Irena, would you ask Father to join us? Be discreet."

"Adam, Rihard is a fan of yours and is most interested in the field of architecture."

"So?"

"Yes, he has dreams of being an architect."

"Very admirable on your part, son."

Irena entered the room, followed by the long-legged priest.

"Father," Leona continued, "We need your input in this conversation. Rihard is most interested in taking classes in architecture, but I fear that none are being offered in this area. Dr. Wiadek is a professor of architecture; I was wondering if we couldn't possibly make a match somehow?"

Wiadek leaned back in his chair and adjusted his prince-nez; the plot was about to unfold.

"Are you currently teaching in the underground university, Professor?"

"As a matter of fact, I am Father. I conduct an advanced class in Praga, one night a week, but I wouldn't reject the idea of teaching a beginning class here in Warsaw, if I had a secure place and a large enough group of students to warrant my time and effort."

"I can offer you a safe haven on Wednesday nights, in the basement of the church, where Professor Bednarek holds her classes in history. The students could be conjured up. A bulletin will be prepared with a coded message of an additional class being offered and I will get my angels to promote the idea within the Grey Ranks."

"Very well, Father, you come up with a suitable class size and I'll come up with a curriculum."

# CHAPTER 26

Dr. Wiadek's class on Architecture managed to attract enough students to make his curriculum of instruction worthwhile. The northwest corner of the church basement offered a weekly home for Architecture 101. Rihard Borowski, his first student, felt obligated to perform well. He and another member of the class, Stevik Mieleski, met routinely at one of the many coffee houses that sprung up in Warsaw. Wiadek was a disciplined pedantic, and they needed to be well prepared.

Stevik arrived at the coffee house earlier than usual. A pool table was set up in the backroom to provide some diversion for the bored youth of the city. Governor Fischer looked on it as a means of keeping the rebellious youth busy until curfew and diminish the opportunities for sabotage. Stevik took his cup of coffee and settled at a table to observe the ongoing game.

Borowski soon joined him and ordered a small coffee.

"Who have you placed your bet on this week, Stevik?"

"I haven't, yet; I'm observing the strategy of the players before I make a judgment. Rihard, see that fellow in the blue rolled neck sweater?" Stevik did not take his eyes from his friend's face as Borowski scanned the room.

"Yes."

"I have seen him on occasion with Wiadek. Do you suppose he's his bodyguard?"

"Could be. He certainly looks the type. Why don't you engage him in a game?"

"I think I will." Stevik left his seat and carefully maneuvered his way around the pool table, ostensibly to follow the ball, until he came upon the muscle-bound man in the blue sweater.

He waited until the balls were racked up before he spoke.

"Are you good at the game?"

"Oh, I'm sure I could break the balls in a decent pattern," He did not look up from the end of the stick he held in his hand as he rubbed it with chalk.

"If there's time; will you take me on?"

The player placed the stick within the proper finger-hold of his right hand that gripped the table edge, he did not look up. "My time is limited tonight, but if you meet me here on Friday, I'll take you up on a game."

"What time, Friday?"

"Three o'clock. That way we might get a spot at the table."

"By the way," he offered his hand, "I'm Stevik."

"Andrje." He laid the stick on the table and took a good look at his future opponent as they shook hands.

"See you on Friday Andrje."

The balls were clacking loudly in the back room of the coffee house. Stevik was prepared to wait for the game to end. He ordered a cup of coffee and followed the noise to the pool table.

Andrje was the only one there. Stevik watched intently as the lone player executed a difficult shot with his left hand. The stick propelled two balls into opposite directions. The balls obediently followed the stroke and landed in separate pockets at the end of the table.

"Andrje, I thought there was a game in progress."

"I'm taking practice shots. I don't know how good my adversary is."

Stevik laughed, "Oh, I'm sure I could break the balls in a decent pattern."

"Touché, my friend, touché."

They managed to get in two sets before the room filled with other gamers waiting to get a chance at the table. Stevik made a good showing, but he was no match for an obvious pool sharp.

"Let's get out of here." Andrje plucked his cap from the hat rack. "We'll go to the Nectar, and I'll treat you to a consolation prize."

During the walk to the restaurant, Stevik tried to hit on a topic of conversation that might prove to be of mutual interest.

"My friend, Rihard was unable to accompany me today. He's a ten hour a day employee at the Labor Office."

Andrje made no comment, nor did he acknowledge the report by any gesture. He seemed unwilling to engage in conversation, and the pair walked the six blocks in silence.

Most of the personnel of the Nectar were members of the underground. There was little that went on that escaped their notice.

The waitress and Andrje engaged in a familiarity that was obviously an ongoing flirtation. They went to the bar for a *Na zdrovia*. Before Andrje raised his glass, he lowered his chin, lifted his eyes, and looked directly at Stevik.

"Listen, little brother," he pointed a finger his way, "I know when I'm being manipulated. You're not that good a pool player to take me on. You saw me play. You made it your business to try to make my acquaintance."

Still wet behind the ears; Stevik felt as though he were playing with the big boys. His eyes widened and he stared at Andrje.

"No, really, I admired your skill and I wanted to see if I could hold my own in a game with you. You're right. It was stupid. Sometimes my head's too big."

Andrje leaned back in his seat.

"What do you and your friend do on Wednesday nights?" He downed his vodka, "I see you coming into the coffee house at the same time every week for over a month now, and you leave at precisely five o'clock."

"We come to watch the pool games."

Andrje plunked his glass down on the table with a thud and grabbed his cap.

"See you on Wednesday."

Professor Adam Wiadek was gainfully employed as a clerk in the Nazi Administration's City Planning and Development Office. The foreign occupiers were on an entirely different tract from the pre-war operation of the city. The Germans were focusing their attention on the eventual establishment of Hitler's plans for *Lebensraum*.

The Nazis held little interest in the antiquated documents pertaining to Warsaw's development. The maps and deeds of the past remained on the archive's shelves, gathering dust. Wiadek was privy to these plans. His interest in the archives was specifically oriented to the maps of pre-war Poland. These documents contained detailed plans of the original street addresses and the important buildings and landmarks of Warsaw.

Dysthmus pulled up to the covert garage maintained by the Home Army. Both doors of the dark green Opel Kapitan opened at once. Dysthmus and the champion pool player, Andrje, hopped out of the car and hurried into the building.

K-Division had carjacking down to a science. Within the garage, several German Lorries had received dramatic makeovers. Two of them were painted a dull gray with large black letters on the side panels revealing them to be delivery trucks for office products. Dysthmus took the wheel of one of the Lorries with Andrje in the passenger seat.

The truck proceeded into Center City, then wound around to the back entrance of the City Planning and Development Office.

The two men emerged from the truck and were greeted at the door by Dr. Wiadek. There was a minimum of conversation as several large cartons were removed from the building and stashed within the truck.

The loaded vehicle curved along the northern backroads for some thirty kilometers. They approached a dense forest and cut across a roughly hewn road, which owed its origin to the heavy vehicles that continuously wound their way over the brush into the Home Army's Headquarters.

Andrje proceeded to the door of the building with the clipboard that held the itemized list of the cargo. Meanwhile, Dysthmus unlocked the tailgate to begin the unloading of the shipment. Cartons of maps and pertinent documents of Warsaw's City Planning and Development Office would gather dust in their new home. One day, they would provide the diagram for a free and independent Warsaw.

# CHAPTER 27

Kaminski dropped by Michael's office after lunch.

"Come with me Bednarek. A meeting of the magistrates of the Secret Court is scheduled for two-thirty."

"This is sudden. When did you learn of this meeting?"

"Early this morning. Information on clandestine meetings are not sent out ahead of time."

"Give me a few minutes to put my files away."

Kaminski sat in the comfortable client's chair and pulled out his notepad and pencil. He was scribbling an outline for his column when Michal interrupted him.

"Are you ready? I don't want to be late for my first appearance before the magistrates."

Kaminski lifted his pencil mid-sentence, closed his notebook, replaced it in his jacket, squirmed out of his seat, and followed Michal out the door.

"Will we be taking a tram?"

"No, the meeting spot is in walking distance."

They walked along together until they came to Buxom Street.

Kaminski's eyes darted about, scanning the area.

"Okay, we'll separate here. I'll make a quick stop at the distribution center across the street, and you continue on your way to the stationery store." He searched Michal's eyes. "You know Potopski?"

"I know that he's been marked a suspect collaborator."

"Go in and tell him you have need of legal pads for depositions."

Michal's eyebrows raised; a quizzical frown pulled at his forehead.

"Remember that old adage? Believe nothing you hear and only half of what you see." He put his hand on Michal's shoulder. "You're safe. Follow Potopski's instructions. I'll see you later."

He left Michal standing on the corner, perplexed. Was he really ready to invest himself in this sort of espionage? Right from the start he was expected to announce himself to a man who was rumored to be in collaboration with the Nazis. There seemed to be too many twists and turns involved in this covert life style.

He made his way to the stationery store and went in. There was no one in the shop. After a few moments, he felt self-conscious and started to inspect the shelves as if he were looking for something.

"Pan Bednarek."

The sudden call of his name startled him. He turned in the direction of the voice.

"Good afternoon, Edward, I am in need of legal pads."

"I have packages of six; how many will you need?"

"Just the one, thank you."

Potopski brought the package to the register. He smiled broadly as his eyes darted between the two large windows that provided a view of the intersecting streets outside of his shop. Continuing to smile, he addressed his customer in his business-like style.

"Welcome Michal. At the back of the store, you'll find a huge closet. Push the coats aside and you'll find another door that leads to the basement. The light is already on; they're waiting for you."

Too confused to respond, he followed the instructions.

Three sharp pings startled him when he opened the second door. He paused. He could feel the muscles of his neck stiffen in response to the eerie feeling in his stomach. He listened intently; he was sure he heard scuffling down below. He proceeded cautiously down the steps.

"Bednarek, good you could come." An elderly gentleman filed into the center of the floor. Two other figures appeared from behind the tall pillars that served to buttress the foundation of the building.

He recognized a former judge of the Justice System of Poland, Peter Butkowski. Michal was impressed. The judge was held in high esteem within the courts.

Butkowski seated himself at the center of a long table that stood along the back wall. The Honorable Judge had somehow managed to maintain the rugged good looks Michal remembered from his days in the Polish courts. Anton Matewski, another judge from the justice system, years younger than Butkowski, had not fared as well. His skin was sallow, and he had lost a good deal of weight. The barristers at court viewed him as a self-righteous individual who wielded his gavel as a sword. Matewski took the seat to the right of Butkowski.

Michal walked toward the judge and extended his hand. "Your honor, may I say you are looking well."

"For an old warhorse, you mean." He turned his head to acknowledge his colleague.

"You know the Honorable Judge, Anton Matewski."

Michal took his hand, "Your honor."

Butkowski went on with the introductions. "Advocate Albert Pierski. Albert was about to be sworn in as a justice of the lower court, when all hell broke loose."

Michal had worked in opposition to Albert Pierski, the prosecuting attorney in the District Attorney's office. Pierski, handsomely striking with an abundance of blonde hair, was self-confident and debonair. He pulled a chair to the front of the table, offering Michal a ringside seat of the proceedings. "I am well familiar with Michal Bednarek and his compelling gift of delivering a well-prepared defense."

Michal offered a modest smile.

Butkowski opened the meeting. "Attorney Bednarek, we will have a courier bring the document of the rules and procedures of our covert court to your office. It would not be wise to allow you to carry them on your person as you travel the streets. Review them thoroughly and secure them safely, as the document is a matter of top security. We do not have the time to go over the contents during this meeting."

He motioned to Pierski to begin.

"The defendant is one, Lieutenant Lukorski, of the Blue Police. Complaints have been made charging him with brutal treatment of the citizens of Warsaw in the execution of his duties. Allegedly, he has been active in the surveillance and consequent arrest of individuals he suspects of committing acts of disturbance against the General Government." He laid the document in front of him on the table. "At this time, we have enough signed complaints against him to begin proceedings."

Michal was familiar with Lukorski's methods. Several of his previous clients had their fate sealed by this turn-coat officer. The Blue Police consisted of the pre-war Warsaw Police Force. The Germans forced them to cooperate in the maintenance of public order. Lukorski was more compliant than others. A death sentence would be justified.

Pierski looked at Michal. "We have other cases running now, all in different stages of the process. If you could take on the depositions of the people who have signed complaints, we could move this case forward to a conclusion."

"Certainly, give me the list and I'll begin tomorrow."

Butkowski smiled up at him. "Good, as soon as all legal procedures are completed and the Chief Delegate approves the sentence, we'll turn the case over to the K-Division for his execution."

# CHAPTER 28

Corporal Maximillian Hegler jotted down the message as he received it over the phone. A prosperous Schindlerite was interested in purchasing a confiscated estate in Mokotow, a suburb of Warsaw. The manor house was at least three-hundred years old, and the prospective owner was interested in obtaining a history of the property. Dr. Wiadek, Hegler's supervisor was at lunch.

The corporal was familiar with the catalogued list of registered deeds, itemized according to lot number and dates of purchase. The documents dated back to the early years of the tenth century. He could have the required information sitting on the chief's desk before he returned from his break. All he had to do was find the right box on the right shelf.

Professor Wiadek's Wednesday night architectural class slipped into a noisy social gathering as the minutes ticked by and Dr. Wiadek did not appear for the lesson. At twenty minutes past the hour, several students became anxious. Borowski volunteered to go to Dr. Bednarek's class to inquire about the unusual circumstances.

He hesitated at her door. How would she react to his interruption?

Leona noticed him peering into the room and went to the doorway. "Yes, what is it, Rihard?"

"Professor Wiadek has not arrived, and there is growing concern."

She paused a moment, to gain control, and then answered smoothly.

"Yes—Rihard, uh, the professor has a meeting this evening. Obviously, something went wrong in the communication network and the class was not informed."

She turned around to address her class. "Excuse me, I need to leave the room a moment, please continue with your journaling."

Rihard followed her into Wiadek's room.

"Class, there has been some gross misunderstanding. Dr. Wiadek is engaged in a very important meeting and will not be lecturing this evening. I apologize for the inconvenience. Class is dismissed."

Her history session seemed to drag on interminably. She did not allow time for questioning after dismissal. "Please, make a note of your questions and comments and we will go over them before we begin the lesson, next week." She quickly gathered her books and hurried Irena out of the building and onto the street in her rush to get home.

A sliver of light stretched across the carpet in front of Michal's study; he was still at work. She left Irena in the foyer.

"Michal, there is a serious problem with Adam Wiadek. He never showed up for class tonight."

Michal's hands remained on the spreadsheet before him as he stared into space.

"Michal!"

"Yes, dear, I hear you." He looked at his watch, "Curfew. We'll just have to wait until morning."

Michal made his usual breakfast stop at the Center Café. He ordered coffee and waited for Kaminski to appear and assuage his concern. Kaminski's failure to show served to increase his angst. It was growing late; he would have to leave if he was to open his office for the day.

Kaminski had no time for breakfast. He sat at his desk, banging away at the typewriter. He hadn't been to bed. He spent the night printing the weekly issue of The Polish Journal.

# PROMINENT ARCHITECT, DR. ADAM WIADEK ARRESTED

By the time Michal returned home at the end of the day, everyone in Warsaw knew of the arrests. The Gestapo had blared out the news over the loudspeakers that hung over the major streets of the city.

He found Leona correcting the daily journals her students kept documenting their lives under the Nazi regime.

"Your journaling and teaching must cease!"

She looked up at him, startled by the sharp tone he used to address her.

"Wiadek's gone! You'll be next!"

Janina entered the room before Leona could respond.

"Pani, would you rather potatoes or *kluski* for dinner this evening?"

Leona pursed her lips to hold back a smile. Janina had never sought her advice about dinner.

"I leave that to you, Janina. Thank you for asking."

She turned to Michal, "The Flying University is an age-old establishment of Poland. We professors know the risk we take. We also know what can become of a country without an intelligencia. Wiadek's sacrifice reflects the thousands of martyred teachers that came before him and will continue to come as long as one nation is bent upon the destruction of another."

Michal stood there, absorbing the impact of her speech. He made a valiant effort to ignore the feeling of dissolution that took hold of him. He took a deep breath, shook his head and left the room.

The usual low-keyed hum of conversation was absent at the café. There was a marked variation of behavior among the breakfast crowd. The Schindlerites were boisterously conversing, while the Warszawians maintained a dull murmur at their tables. Wiadek's arrest was still the topic of interest.

Michal waited patiently, while Kaminski performed his gregarious entrance.

"Have you any information on Wiadek?"

"Nothing I can verify, just yet. Genowefa was arrested also. Rumor has it they are no longer at Szucha Street."

Michal turned pale. Kaminski went on, "It seems they are on their way to Paviak."

"Zygmunt, I'm most concerned about Leona. She may be next!"

"Don't over-react, Michal. He was not arrested for teaching. His offense is far greater than that. He has stolen documents from the archive of the Nazi administration. It's a capital offense. The Wiadeks are not expected to remain guests of the Gestapo much longer."

# CHAPTER 29

The Nazi's pursuit of the Bacchanalian good life allowed the insurgents the ways and means to conduct clandestine meetings. Warsaw had a wide variety of restaurants and coffee houses to satisfy the German palate and pursuit of the vine.

The Nectar catered to the Germans. Since the occupation, Sauerbraten and sauerkraut had become a specialty of the house, and several German beers were on tap. The restaurant was staffed by partisans of the underground, who were united in a common cause. Each and every one of them had suffered the loss of family members or friends under the Nazi regime. Revenge fueled their rebellion. Individually and collectively, they could be counted on to maintain silence of anything on toward that came their way.

Kaminski decided on a change of venue for lunch. His usual choice was for a home cooked meal at the restaurant of a former comedic actress who was also renowned as a great chef of Polish cuisine. The Chestnut was where he hung his hat at the end of the day, usually sitting at the bar chatting with his confidant, Jashek, the bartender. On this particular evening, he had a yen for the Nectar's specialty of the house, the German style stuffed breast of veal. The dish was a regular treat in his mother's kitchen back in Poznan; comfort food to a boy of mixed heritage. A hearty glass of beer would top off the meal.

He was on a first name basis with many of the German patrons of the Nectar. His command of their language and his stylish mode of dress earned him a dubious respect among the Schindlerites.

Anna, the hostess, interrupted his usual kibitzing in the lobby to escort him to his table. They exchanged a bit of chit-chat as she handed him the menu. He glanced over the specialties in the off chance that something unfamiliar might tempt his palate. He sensed the waitress hovering over him and looked up.

"May I take your order, sir?"

Pola Duzat, dressed in the uniform of a waitress, stood with pad and pencil in her hands.

Much to his relief, they managed the order process in a business-like manner. Nothing transpired between them that would reveal the fact that they knew one another.

Later that evening he stopped by Kazek's bar for a drink. Dysthmus was perched on a stool at the bar, and Kaminski joined him.

"I had lunch at the Nectar, this afternoon."

"Aha! You were surprised by the lovely new waitress."

"What is she doing in town?"

"She is living in town, at the Piantak residence, no less."

Kaminski offered a confused expression, and Dysthmus continued.

"The formerly wealthy Piantaks are family. Anna and she are close in age and get along well."

Kaminski, not to be put off, reiterated, "What is she doing in town?"

"She is in the middle of her Home Army courses in disruption and sabotage through D-Division. She wants to be a hero like her brother Felix." There was a note of disdain in his final remark. He finished his drink and stood up. "I have to go."

Kaminski made the obvious connection.

Anna Piantak was the popular hostess at the Nectar. She ushered her patrons to their table with a grace and fluidity that was not overlooked. A member of the gentry, she had studied ballet for years and had appeared on the stage. That life was behind her now, as it was for most artists in Warsaw. The theatre was governed by the Germans, and any involvement in the entertainment business was construed as collaboration. Many actors and musicians found work as waiters and staff in the restaurants and coffee houses that dotted Center City.

Obviously, Pola had approached her for help, and Anna responded by providing a place for her in her father's home, along with a job at the restaurant.

When Dysthmus heard she was working at the Nectar, he went directly to the Piantak home to confront her. The place still had an air of grandeur about it, but it suffered from advancing age. Many of the rooms had been closed in an effort to economize power and fuel. Daily housekeeping tasks were performed in lackluster fashion by the inept family members, who had lived their entire lives being cared for by servants.

Pan Christopher Piantak, himself, opened the door to Dysthmus.

"Good evening, Pan. I'm here to visit your new border, Pola Duzat."

The old man gave a weak smile and a little nod of his head. With a stately bearing, he led his guest through the hall and into the living room.

"Please, Marek, do be seated, and I will see if she is at home."

He remained standing.

Somehow, the family had managed to hold onto some costly antique furniture, but the priceless collection of books, the elegant ceramics and works of art were conspicuously absent.

He did not wait long.

Pola entered the room alone. "*Kochanek!*"

She threw herself at him.

His posture stiffened and he pushed her away.

"Have you lost your mind?" he snapped, "You're a child; you belong at home with your parents. And what about your grandmother; hasn't she lost enough?"

"I'm eighteen! I'm not a child!"

"Your family considers you to be their child. Pola, the Germans are savages. Here, in Warsaw, you're in constant danger. On the farm, you're surrounded by family and relatively safe."

"There is no safe place in Poland. No safe place in Europe. I have to do what my heart tells me."

"What are you, Joan of Arc?"

His final remark and the hostile attitude he presented were unexpected and stung. She broke down and cried.

He stared at the bowl of wax fruit on the huge tea table, while he sorted out anger from compassion. Once his genuine feelings settled his dilemma, the anger subsided, and he reached out to her. He put his arms around her, and she snuggled into his embrace. The physical contact loosened barriers; they clung to one another and let the tears flow.

The sobbing and heavy sighs subsided. Dysthmus loosened his grip—he lifted her chin and kissed her lips. Pola responded a bit too sensuously and he was in danger of committing an action, and himself, to an impulse that was bound to have irrevocable consequences. He responded by resorting to his initial feelings of anger.

He pulled away. "Go home! If you stay, you're just one more responsibility, and I have enough to deal with."

# CHAPTER 30

The certificate of completion was signed, dated, and issued to "Kwiatek," Pola's code name. Her practicum was under the tutelage of Borza, a seasoned veteran of underground diversion. She would be the only messenger Pola would ever come to know during her service. The identity of the other liaison girls would remain secret. Women caught delivering messages would undergo interrogation, torture and death. The anonymity of those involved in the unit provided some security for the continued success of the mission.

Middle-aged, and full of energy, Borza's role in the division was comparable to a major of the military. She had a deep voice and she spoke her instructions in a slow and measured pattern.

"There are two entities within the network. Normal and Rush. The Normal service requires a great deal of caution, and there are no time constraints. Guarantee of delivery is the consideration." She paused and looked Pola in the eye, before continuing to lay out the procedures.

Pola scribbled notes on a pad.

"Rush is exactly what the word implies. They deliver a warning of arrests or eminent danger to the individual or division. These messages are trusted to liaison girls who have been proven efficient and fearless." She looked over at the pad in Pola's lap.

"Read from your notes."

Pola gave a nervous account of her jottings.

"Are there any questions?"

Pola shook her head.

"You understand, then?"

Pola nodded.

Borza pulled a small sheet of paper out of her jacket pocket. "This is the list of deposit boxes that are distributed throughout Warsaw." She handed the list to Pola.

"Four sectors are allocated to the city. The addresses for the boxes are listed. If for some reason, you are unable to deliver your message, drop it off at the nearest sector and the person in charge will see to its proper delivery." She waited until Pola raised her eyes from the list.

"Kwiatek, you are to memorize the list. Store it in a safe place until you have it committed to memory, then discard it."

Borza supervised the first few missions. The messages were the usual war slogans; unimportant trivia trusted to the novice. On her first independent assignment, Borza followed a short distance behind. Fear and tension do not accommodate successful espionage exercises. Pola could not remember exactly where her first drop was located. Borza reprimanded her and told her to check her list, only to discover that the novitiate had destroyed it after she felt sure she had it memorized. Borza left her at the site and did not contact her again.

Felix was on her mind more than ever. Images of the two of them running through the barns and neglecting their chores came upon her at the oddest moments. Memories of his constant taunting of the crush she had on Marek brought smiles, not blushes. These childhood memories were savored when they occurred. They served as a balm to offset the gnawing feeling of guilt she felt at the dark moments of the day. Shame at failing her division, her nation, and Felix would thrust her into a brown study.

Eventually, Pola put duty above pride and contacted Borza. She had to regain her sense of purpose; she had to serve her mission. Borza was not available to her. All of her efforts were ignored; too much was at stake to risk a failed message drop. Re-instatement became an obsession with her. She spent her free time wandering through the shops and stores of the city to explore back exits for quick escapes. Somehow, her preoccupation paid off. She was summoned to meet with Borza. The list was once more presented, along with an admonition; the addresses were to be memorized as well as she knew the Pater Nostra.

Without her knowledge, a member of D-Division tracked her for the first few deliveries. During the final test, the tracker allowed herself to be noticed by Pola, and behaved in a covert manner, assuming the demeanor of a spy.

Pola slipped down a side street and paused to look in a shop window. The agent also turned the corner and casually stopped to light a cigarette. Pola slipped inside the shop and began to inspect the merchandise. A clerk came up to her to suggest possible items.

"Is there another exit?" she asked the clerk.

"Yes, follow me."

Pola escaped out the back door that led to Marszalowska Street, the main thoroughfare of Warsaw. She hopped on the first passing tram. Once she felt sure that she had lost her shadow, she got off and boarded the next tram traveling in the opposite direction, to return to the area where she was to make her drop.

Her tracker waited at the stop for the anticipated return. She continued to follow Pola, this time at a surreptitious distance behind to witness the successful drop-off. Her report detailed the quick thinking and follow through of her mission, and Pola was granted the title Liaison Girl, Kwiatek.

# CHAPTER 31

Pola took the early morning train into Sochaczew so that she could join the family at mass.

In the kitchen, after mass, Kielbasa and eggs were stirred up along with song in the loud and clear voices of the Duzat women. The songs were mostly hymns; some were old ditties that told of romantic love that didn't last. The usual bawdy medleys that bounced off the walls in the past were retired for the duration.

Ludwiga stopped singing and turned her attention to Pola.

"How is Uncle Christopher?"

Pola gave some thought to the question before she decided to answer truthfully.

"He's not doing well, Bapca. He's lost so much weight. He has little appetite, and he is always so sad."

The old woman accepted the report; it was as she suspected.

"And you, my little one; how are you?" Her tone was heartfelt. She knew not to appear concerned, as this might ward off any spontaneous response from her granddaughter.

"I'm glad I have off this Sunday, so I can spend it with you, Bapca." She gave Ludwiga a kiss on the cheek.

There was something of an unsettled nature hovering over the farm. Her father's smiles were weak and forced; she noticed more lines on his forehead, more gray hairs pushing through the sideburns.

Aunt Halina laid a place on the table by Felix' empty chair.

Uncle Vitzek's speech was reduced to yes and no. At times, he would merely nod his head.

The meal was on the table and Ludwiga was about to say grace, when they heard a car pull into the driveway. Ludwiga went on with the prayer. Fredryk made the sign of the cross and rose from the table.

The family waited until the unexpected visitor was at the door.

"Praise be Jesus Christ."

"Forever and ever." Ludwiga smiled softly.

Vitzek nodded his head; Halina and Matcha rose from the table and greeted Dysthmus with a kiss.

"Sit." Fredryk commanded as walked over to the cupboard for a plate and setting.

Ludwiga seemed to be the only one to notice the awkward silence that occurred between Marek and Pola. As he sat down, he glanced at her granddaughter and gave a nod. Pola lowered her eyes and did not respond.

"What's news in the city?" Fredryk asked.

"The newly appointed chief delegate, Jankowski, is juggling all of the resistance organizations without dropping a one. Civil resistance continues; unfortunately, so does the starvation of citizens."

"What kind of minds choose to punish innocent children in such a way? Is there no end to the savage manner the Germans impose on us?" Vitzek responded.

Silence hovered like a cloud over the table.

Marek made an effort to move things along, "And how goes it on the farm?" He looked directly at Fredryk.

Vitzek answered, "The quota managers are making it very difficult for farmers to pinch away any produce. They have charts and graphs to measure the yield. And they do this on a regular basis, to be exact in their accounts for the harvest."

Pola looked at her uncle in dismay. He had always operated in total compliance with the German edicts.

Marek made it a point to direct his next question, "Fredryk, is there any way to get around this?"

"We have been batting this about. The Peasant Battalion has come up with only one resolution. We must destroy the documents."

Fredryk noticed the look of shock on his daughter's face. He changed the subject, "Here, have some more kielbasa."

Ludwiga and Halina cleared away the breakfast dishes and Matcha took her daughter outside. Their visits were short and infrequent, and Matcha was beginning to resent the lack of intimacy between them.

"Pola, please, tell me truthfully; how are things in the city?"

"Mama, I'm kept so busy, I don't have time to think about much."

"And your job in the Nectar; is that exciting?"

"Yes, Mama, it is." A playful look played about her eyes, and she smiled broadly.

"The men pay so much attention to me!"

"Pola that is not a good thing. You know why men behave that way!" She searched her daughter's face. "Is there someone that interests you?"

"Not in the way you mean, Mama, but there is a very handsome young lieutenant that makes my stomach jump."

"A Nazi?"

"He's not like the others, Mama. But you don't need to worry; I know better."

"Then why all this interest?"

"Because he frightens me Mama. Not because he is a Nazi, but because of the way he makes me feel when I'm near him."

Fredryk called to them from the porch door. "Come, Marek leaves now."

Dysthmus approached her. "I'll drive you home."

"I have a return ticket."

"Save it. The ride is on me."

"I have to pack my things." She ran into the house.

Matcha pulled him to the side. "Marek, I'm very worried about Pola. She has the body of a woman and the emotional make up of a child."

He grimaced and nodded his head.

"Please, Marek, do watch out for her. She's not in command of her feelings toward men."

Conversation was limited on the way back to Warsaw. Pola mumbled her concern over the unseemly turn of events that had her father and uncle sharing the same point of view regarding the Nazi quotas. She caught his eye and held it, "They are involved in the Peasant Battalion, aren't they?"

"You are not the only one to be affected by the death of Felix."

His remark left her to ponder the situation, as well as its significance. She remained silent during the ride home in the Opel. They pulled up to the Piantak's drive. Dysthmus got out of the car and walked around to the passenger side to open the door for Pola. She thanked him and reached for her bag.

"I'll get that." They remained silent during the short walk to the door, it was already curfew. The Piantak parlor was empty. The family had retired for the night. Dysthmus laid her bag on the floor and bent down to kiss her head. "Good night."

She lifted her face and caught the kiss on her lips. She put her arms around his neck and held the kiss. Their breathing grew rapid; she moved her fingers through his hair and pressed against his loin. He tightened his grip and reached for the zipper at the back of her dress; it ran the length of her torso, he reached in to feel the soft cloth of panties that covered her firm buttocks. The intensity of the petting went beyond the point of caution. He lifted her from the floor and carried her to the divan.

# CHAPTER 32

The windows were open to catch the early morning breeze. Grot awoke to the chirping of birds in the trees that surrounded the house on Spiska Street.

On rare occasions, he was able to take up residence in the house; he came and went suitably attired as a man of business. Spiska Street offered a refuge where he could indulge himself with creature comforts, so woefully curtailed by life in the military. It had been weeks since he was treated to a refreshing night's rest.

He reached over to the night table and glanced at his watch, eight o'clock; he had overslept. He enjoyed the feeling of the relaxed pace and rolled over on his back to mentally review his duties of the day. June 30, there was a meeting at ten that morning. Chief Delegate Jankowski had called the meeting to discuss the fiscal budget. The Home Army would be first in line for future expenditures.

He rose from the bed, jiggled his feet into a pair of leather slippers and made his way to the shower.

Downstairs, Jetka, his aide-de-camp, was rattling pots and pans. The aroma of contraband coffee and frying onions aroused the general's appetite. He would hurry with his shower and be downstairs before Jetka called.

Rowecki had the newspaper propped up by the coffeepot. This would be his only chance to review the latest German propaganda. A coded knock on the front door interrupted breakfast. Jetka rose from the table and walked to the door. He looked through the peephole before turning the latch.

The general sipped his coffee; while he waited, he gave a cursory glance at the *Nowy Kourier*. He nodded to himself when he heard Jetka close the door. He was expecting a package to be delivered by courier.

"A liaison girl dropped this off."

"Thank you." From the expression of relief that showed on his face, Jetka half expected the general to say, "Thank God!"

He took the bundle, wrapped in newspaper, and made his way to the dining room. He placed it on the table while he removed a hidden panel from the commode. He squeezed the package into the empty space, and then replaced the panel.

"It's almost nine-thirty, Sir."

"Yes, I know Jetka. I'm running late. I'm lingering—hate to end this short respite." He started for the stairs. "I have only to finish grooming and I'll be off."

The blare of sirens blasted in the street. At least fifty Gestapo cars screeched their brakes, and over two hundred men began to invade every house on the street. Brown shirts were swarming on the rooftops. The residents were forced from their homes and herded into a cordoned off area in the street.

The door to the Spiska Street hideout was battered down and a group of SS men barged in on Grot before he could run for the secret exit.

He was shackled, removed from the premises, and shoved into one of the cars.

Jozef Lypka, a janitor in the Gestapo headquarters on Szucha Street, left his bucket and mop in a corner and ran to find out what all the excitement was about. Triumphant shouts were heard ringing out in the halls and stairwell. Jozef, with his limited understanding of German, was able to make out, "Death of the underground!" and the name of "Grot." Another, unfamiliar name, "General Rowecki," was also being tossed about. Lypka paid this no mind. His concern was over the alarming news of the capture of his hero. Every citizen of Warsaw knew the name of General Grot; he was looked upon as the venerable protector of Poland.

Jozef looked at the clock, ten minutes past eleven. There was another twenty minutes until his lunch break. He knew where to find Kaminski.

He put his bucket and mop away, grabbed his time ticket, and clocked out. Would he make it back within his allotted half-hour break?

He rushed along the streets and ran up the steps to the Chestnut Café. Kaminski wasn't there. He brushed past the hostess and went straight to the bar.

"I must see Kaminski!" he announced to the bartender.

Jashek gave him a stern look, "What for?"

"I must see Kaminski."

"Well, he's not here. Give me a message and I'll deliver it to him—if he comes."

Jozef delivered a defiant look.

"Look, you beggar, people are coming in for lunch. I can't have you hanging around the bar. Now, you've got to get out of here."

Jozef stood there, wringing his cap in his hands. His lips moving rapidly as he silently prayed to the Virgin. Jashek pulled him behind the bar and was shoving him toward the back entrance when the old man caught sight of Kaminski entering the lobby. He wrenched himself free and ran toward him.

Kaminski reacted smoothly. Lypka was his Szucha Street informant.

"Ah, Jozef, I have need of you. My office needs a good cleaning." He walked him out the door, and onto the street, where he drew a few kopeks out of his pocket and handed them to the janitor in case any of the diners were watching from the window.

"They have captured Grot!"

This time, Kaminski did not respond as quickly. He had difficulty processing the information.

"They have him locked up in one of the confined cells."

"I wondered why he didn't show for the meeting," he muttered. "Do you know which cell it is, Jozef?"

"Yes, it's one they use for the solitary confinement. It's well-guarded."

# CHAPTER 33

Kaminski's first notion was to check with Virski, but he had no idea where Virski went after the meeting. He would have to seek out Kumor, in K-Division.

He arrived at the hideout and was allowed entrance. Once inside, he was totally ignored. Everyone in the building was focused on their specific task. He stood in a corner and observed the bustle.

He finally caught sight of Kumor rushing through the hall.

"Kumor, what's the latest on Grot?"

"The news has been transmitted to the government in London. Sikorski is still in the Middle East, inspecting the Polish Troops. The message has been directed to General Sosnkowski, to be relayed to the premier."

Kaminski jotted down the comments.

"That's all the information I can give you. You must leave, as we have much to do which is top security. Deputy Commander Komorowski is resuming command.

The first thing on the top security list was to disperse a recovery team to Spiska Street. They were specialists in breaking into discovered hideouts to remove hidden items and documents. They were accompanied by the carpenter who designed the secret niches and panels at the Spiska residence.

The Gestapo had already gone through the dwelling and had sealed the doors and windows. The team had no trouble breaking the seals. They went through the dwelling in a precise pattern that could have been choreographed. The Nazis had uncovered nothing; the items were well hidden. The team left the area as they had found it, re-sealed the door, and escaped through the garden.

The newspaper wrapped bundle, delivered by the liaison girl that morning, contained fifteen thousand American dollars.

A second team was involved in the rescue operation. Thanks to Jozef Lypka, they knew the exact location of their prisoner. Several plans were discussed and abandoned. Finally, a plot was put forth that won approval. A German vehicle under repair in the Gestapo garage would be filled with explosives. Volunteers, who understood the inevitable outcome of their suicide mission, would ram it into the building. As soon as the effects of the blast had settled, another team would rush in to remove Rowecki.

The plan was never put to the test. The K-Division agent assigned the surveillance of Szucha Street, reported that Rowecki had been removed from the premises and was enroute to Berlin.

Count Tadeusz Komorowski's aristocratic lineage went back to the fifteenth century. The king of Hungary granted his ancestors a large property in the hills of southern Poland along with the title. An unexpected change in the will left the property to his father's sister. This bit of legal action deprived the young count of his expected place in the line of inheritance and in doubt of his future. His godfather advised him to join the military and make a career for himself.

By 1938 he was ready to retire from the military. He had served the Polish Army for twenty- five years, fought in the Great War and commanded a cavalry unit in the 1920 war between Poland and Russia. His wife's family estate in Swirz needed tending and he looked forward to the life of a landed gentry. Adolf Hitler put an end to the plan.

He became involved in the organization of the underground militia of the Home Army out of Cracow. Sikorski nominated him Deputy Commander to Rowecki and transferred him to Warsaw at the end of July 1941.

On July 1, 1943, he signed the oath of office and assumed command of the Home Army. The Information Bulletin issued his notice of command, the first document to appear with his official signature, "Commander Bor."

On July 4, 1943, the loudspeakers, installed by the Nazi propaganda machine, blasted the streets of Warsaw.

"ACHTUNG! GENERAL WLADYSLAW SIKORSKI HAS BEEN KILLED IN A PLANE CRASH OVER GIBRALTOR

Sikorski had fought along-side Marshal Pilsudski in the 1919-1920 war that defeated the Red Army; he was reputed to be a brilliant military strategist. Along with his combined authority as Premier and Commander in Chief of the exiled government, Sikorski wore a third hat; he was a skillful diplomat. He had somehow managed to cooperate with Stalin. The Allied Commanders, Roosevelt and Churchill, considered him a forthright and flexible person. He was well liked.

The news exploded over the airways and in the press. Many newspapers across the western world hinted at possible assassination attempts. The German headlines heralded the end of the exiled government of Poland.

# CHAPTER 34

Michal Bednarek was summoned to a meeting of the secret court. K-Division, the intelligence and propaganda unit of the Home Army had uncovered the individuals responsible for the arrest of Rowecki. Death warrants for the traitors had to be drafted and signed by the chief delegate.

The two judges, Butkowski and Matewski took their seats at the center of the table. Albert Pierski, the prosecuting attorney, and Bednarek who served as defense council, completed the seating arrangement. In the middle of the table, a bible and a crucifix set the stage for the inauspicious proceedings about to take place.

Pierski presented the information that was gleaned by K-Division.

"General Rowecki's betrayers were from his own ranks of the Home Army. A trio of double-agents had infiltrated his forces. Ludwig Kalkstein/Stolinski, code name 'Hanka,' a twenty-three-year-old man, was arrested by the Gestapo in 1942. During his internment, he was indoctrinated to the Nazi program. Facing a death penalty by the firing squad, he converted. His new-found loyalty was reinforced by the promise of rewards and possible up-ward mobility in the military." He handed the first document to Butkowski.

Pierski went on, "His wife, Blanka nee Kaczorowska, code name 'Sroka,' and his brother- in-law, Eugeniusz Swierczewski, code name 'Genes,' were persuaded to follow his example."

Butkowski speculated, "Rowecki may not have been their only victim. There have been a number of top military and political arrests and deaths in a short period of time. It seems, the Gestapo is resolved to eliminate the leaders of the resistance."

Pierski concluded, "We suspect that Kalkstein is still in Warsaw, but is being held in security by the Gestapo. His wife, Blanka, is hiding out in the home of her parents. She is quite pregnant. As yet, there is no information on Swierczewski."

The death warrant was typed by Pierski. The document was then signed by the officiating magistrates and sent by courier to the chief delegate for his signature.

A team of special agents from K-Division maintained an around the clock surveillance on the house at 74 Krochmalna Street, the residence of Swierczewski. He was seized the first time he dared to approach his home and dragged to the basement.

The chief operative pronounced the sentence which he read from the official document, signed by the chief delegate. Swierczewski was hung from the rafters of his basement.

Kalkstein remained embedded in the security of the Nazi Administration.

Blanka Kalkstein avoided the death sentence due to her pregnant condition.

All of Poland was in flux. Within one week the exiled government and the commander of the Home Army had changed hands. During the four years of Gestapo rule, the Germans subjugated the population to a ceaseless game of roulette; the Poles never knew at which moment the needle would point their way. The chances of being herded into a roundup for retribution or being shot in a street skirmish was the same for everyone. The glue that kept the fabric together and united them as a nation, was their trust in the exiled government in London and the military at home. Warsaw was governed by two well-structured administrations, Sikorski's exiled government from London, and the German General Government from Berlin. The Poles had chosen to follow Sikorski's edicts, while feigning compliance to the harsh demands of the Nazis occupation.

The shattered Secret State endured the shock wave throughout the myriad of organizations that operated under the umbrella of the Council of National Unity. Maintaining a coherent environment within these diverse organizations held top priority for heads of the underground administration.

Representatives of the organizations began filing into the selected hideout in Czerniakow, a suburb of Warsaw. Chief Delegate Jankowski had called for a meeting; morale was low, and the population needed reassurance.

General Bor's report of the strength of the Home Army was meant to assuage any concerns they may have after Rowecki's capture. Three-hundred thousand sworn members filled the ranks. The larger portion were average citizens living within their communities. They were on call for any emergency that might need their attention. Available around the clock, was a small group of paid professionals who performed the tasks that demanded a higher level of skill. The fighting military, living in the forest and fighting the Germans whenever the occasion arose, comprised the rest of the aggregate. All three-hundred thousand were under Bor's direct control.

Jankowski summed up the future agenda of the governing power in London and the underground Secret State. Stanislaw Mikolajczyk replaced Sikorski as the Second Prime Minister in Exile. Kazimierz Sosnkowski took on Sikorski's role as Commander in Chief; the Government in Exile was alive and well. Plans for an uprising, although still paramount on the list of actions, were currently in a holding pattern, waiting on the judgement of the newly assigned leaders in London. Constant communication remained a mandate. The council would keep the various organizations apprised of any changes that might occur along the way.

Sosnkowski's blood was every bit as blue as Bor's. His father was a land baron of several villages, and a coat of arms was also on display in their villa. Tall and slender, Sosnkowski looked like an aristocrat. He spoke seven languages, and took a lively interest in art, music, politics, and architecture. He was instrumental in designing the battle strategy for the 1920 war against Russia and was a close friend of Pilsudski's.

Along with his analytical mind and sharp intellect came an imperious attitude.

General Bor was under his direct command.

During the customary exit procedure, Kaminski approached Bednarek. "Michal, I haven't seen you since the last meeting. My shop is just down the street. It's early; come join me and I'll reveal my lair to you."

# CHAPTER 35

The journey to the shop turned into a lengthy six blocks. Czerniakow, a blue-collar suburb of Warsaw, housed several industries within the community that provided jobs for skilled workers. Many of the homes had not been maintained for years. There were parts of Czerniakow that exposed a long history of poverty. Kaminski stopped in front of one of the better structures and produced a key to unlock the door. Some basic furnishings occupied the rooms. One small bulb nestled in the ceiling to cast a narrow column of yellow light on the floor. Kaminski led the way to the basement door; he flicked a switch on the wall and the area was flooded with light and the sound of an exhaust fan. They descended a flight of sturdy steps; evidently Kaminski had made some improvements.

Kaminski gestured with his right hand, "This is the home of the Polish Journal."

Shelves lined one long wall. A worktable, a desk, and a hand press printing machine fulfilled the necessary publishing equipment.

"Sometimes, it becomes my home as well. When I'm working late, the work-table becomes my bed."

He walked over to a shelf and reached for a bottle and two glasses. "I have no delightful black-market coffee to offer, but a good host always has a bottle of vodka on hand."

Michal shook his head and smiled.

"Have a seat." Kaminski offered the only chair in the room. "*Na zdrovia!*"

They drank the toast to good health and Kaminski immediately poured another round.

"Well," he raised his glass, "here's to the traitors we have dispersed. The traitorous trio that informed on Grot. May their god welcome them to an eternity in Hell."

He hopped up on the worktable and assumed the tone of a professional story teller.

"Now, I must share with you the latest story I am working on."

"Early this year, the Bureau of Intelligence received a packet of information from Trassenheide, the German Camp in Peenemunde..."

Michael interrupted, "Where is Peenemunde?"

"It's on the Island of Usedom in the Baltic," he moved on, "two Polish prisoners of war, who served as janitors, gathered information of a mysterious weapon the Germans were experimenting with. They managed to gather maps, sketches, and reports of a rocket launching site on the island. Somehow, they smuggled the contents to the Information Bureau."

"These were no ordinary janitors, Zygmunt. They must have been well educated to understand what the plans were about."

"Absolutely. Well, the Bureau gave the packet to a courier to deliver to Churchill. Last week, the RAF raided the living quarters of the scientists; the factory workshop; and" he smiled shrewdly, "the experimental station."

"Does this shut them down?"

"For how long? If this weapon is truly groundbreaking, they'll start again."

He cocked his head to the side, "Unfortunately, the two Polish heroes were unable to escape. They were warned in advance, but there was no air-raid shelter available to the prisoners of the camp, and the SS security was very tight."

"They join the growing list of patriots who give their lives for freedom."

"Michal, I'm going to place an onus on you." He hopped off the table and walked over to his desk. He opened a drawer and removed a small object which he placed in his hand.

"I'm giving you a set of keys to my office. I have no one to inherit my lovely journal. The way the partisans are being wiped out leads me to consider the inevitable possibility of this happening to me, also."

"What will I do with these?"

"You'll become a publisher."

"Zygmunt!"

"Listen, there are times when I must travel outside of Warsaw, not only to sell my paper products, but also to cover important events. Peenemunde is an example. I'm following that story. Meanwhile, things are happening at home that need attention."

He poured another round of vodka.

"I need another journalist to write copy of underground events here, in Warsaw."

"I'm not a journalist. I wouldn't know where to begin."

"I employ a helper, Jerzy. He knows all about you and he will serve you well. He's another one of those patriots who will give their lives to freedom. He will martyr if need be."

"Do I get to meet him?"

"Yes, I'll have him contact you. He extended his hand, "Do I have your hand on this, Michal?"

"Zygmunt, don't get carried away with this, but I'd give my life for you." He took the hand that was offered, and the promise was sealed.

Kaminski threw his head back in a hearty laugh—he quickly sobered, "Do you still have the call-letters to contact Zamski?"

# CHAPTER 36

The aroma of cabbage baking in tomato sauce wafted into the parish garden, where the two priests sat reading The Office, patiently waiting for dinner. Father Pawel took a long sniff. Father Lipinski stifled a smile.

Pani Trypka, the housekeeper, still had the potatoes to mash and the coffee to set perking. The stuffed cabbage she prepared was an "occupation" recipe. She had grown quite adept at revising the old standby recipes she had grown up with. Her long held family recipe required equal amounts of pork and veal to stuff inside the cabbage leaves. Meat had become an unknown substance in the market and the butcher shops. She filled her *golambki* with barley and rice and a fist full of ground chicken breast. The chickens had been former boarders in the garden.

It was traditional for the two old priests to share Thursday night dinners as a celebration of the first Eucharistic Dinner. Father Jan encouraged Trypka to make every effort to serve tempting meals to entice his guest, who seldom ate. Perhaps the fresh tomatoes from the garden would offer an enticement.

At the dinner table, his guest made it a point to take only the amount he was sure he could consume, so as not to leave anything on his plate. After four years of fasting, Father Pawil no longer had the capacity to consume large amounts of food at anyone's table.

Coffee was his only indulgence; he held it as ambrosia and savored it from his saucer like a cat lapping milk. They had their coffee in the library, surrounded by the sweet mold of old and tattered theology books that overflowed the shelves along the walls.

Father Jan spoke haltingly as he puffed to light up the tobacco in his pipe. "So, we are suspended in the air while a new government takes over."

A grim line settled on Father Pawel's lips, "Sikorski had the hearts of all Poles; we trusted him to see us through."

Lipinski pulled on his pipe and reflected, "Not just the Poles, Churchill and Roosevelt respected him. He bent like a willow branch in the wind to follow their opinion of Stalin."

"Mikolajczyk should serve to appease them on that matter."

Newly elected Prime Minister Stanislaw Mikolajczyk's short and stocky stature revealed his peasant roots. Leader of the Peasant Party, he was ardently opposed to the pre-war, quasi-fascist government of Pilsudski. A self-made man, he had the intellectual acuity to learn well from the books he chose for his independently designed curriculum. When he arrived in London in 1940, he challenged himself to learn the English language as quickly as possible. Within a short while he was fluent enough to engage in political discussions with the British administrators, who seemed to understand him despite his heavy accent.

Father Jan reflected, "Let us pray that the peasant and the aristocrat find some mutual ground to agree upon, or Poland will wind up with a dysfunctional governing body." He pulled on the smoke from his pipe and reflected on a scene from the recent past.

"One of the couriers from London, a young man who grew up in this church, had the opportunity to meet with Sosnkowski on a personal level. He invited Mateusz to his home for dinner. He was in Warsaw last week, carrying dispatches for Bor, and he stopped by to see me. Mateusz seemed very impressed by the new C in C's appearance and bearing. According to him, the man is a genius. He speaks seven different languages, including German and Russian. Along with a great intellect he is an artist as well as an architect. On the other side of the coin, Mateusz found him very arrogant. This man will not bend to the peasant, also he regards any attempt to negotiate with Stalin as futile and sure to end in humiliation for the Poles."

Pani Trypka came in to clear away the remaining dishes.

"Father Pawil, you need to get on your way. The last train to Sochaczew leaves in half an hour." She threw a dark look Lipinski's way. "You priests are bound to end up martyrs."

Pawil waited until she left the room. "What is she talking, 'martyrs'?"

"Too many hero deaths. Professor Wiadek's capture and death, and Black Week, have made her anxious about the university classes held in the basement."

"Has she cause to worry?"

Lipinski shrugged a shoulder, "Well, the recent carnage of government and underground officials has had a serious effect on Wednesday night scripture attendance, and all the young students entering the building with such a sparse showing upstairs invites speculation."

"What will you do?"

"I don't know."

# CHAPTER 37

Michal was at the Central Café for breakfast. He no longer cared to break bread at the Napoleon, where he found himself looking toward the door for a grand entrance by Kaminski. He spread a newspaper in front of him and focused on the lies he found in the German propaganda sheet.

"Excuse me, but I think you are Pan Bednarek. I went to school with your daughter, Irena. My name is Jerzy, Jerzy Gruber."

Michal laid yesterday's *Nowy Kourier* on the table and looked up. One of Irena's friends? His appearance suited an SS agent. Tall and very well built, there was an Aryan characteristic about his bearing, something about that blonde hair and blue eyes that expressed a cool intelligence and demanded a certain respect. Should he know him? Surely, he would have remembered this particular friend of Irena's.

"May I join you?"

A nod.

"Ah, the *Nowy Kourier*. I deliver the newspaper all around Warsaw. My route extends to Mokotow and Czerniakow."

What was the association with Czerniakow?

"Jerzy!" The smile of recognition that spread across his face was quickly overcome by an adrenalin rush of foreboding.

"Yes, I have a relative in Czerniakow, my uncle Hienrich, formerly from Lodz."

His direct eye-contact was disconcerting.

Remarks from conversations with Kaminski in the past flooded Michal's thoughts. Hienrich Gruber, a member of the Nazi Party.

He studied the boy as he drank his coffee. Something in his demeanor. His well- articulated speech in a moderate tone had a calming effect.

"Well, I must be on my way. The paper comes off the press at eleven, and I like to finish my route in Czerniakow by three o'clock. That way I have some time to spend with my aunt."

He stood up, "Please extend my well wishes to your daughter."

"Yes." How should he respond? "Ah, umm, I hope to see you again. I have a busy morning. I would love to be finished by three o'clock."

Had he responded correctly? Could he arrange his appointments to clear his calendar in time to be in Czerniakow for a meeting?

If the General Government was considering the proposed sanctions laid out to Father Lipinski during his lunch date with Fischer and Frank, there was no evidence of it. Restrictions and retributions went on as usual.

The crops were ready for harvest and the village managers were making their farm collections. Quota lists, specific to each farm were delivered; there must be no varying of quantities or due dates. Duplicates of the lists—triplicates, were maintained at the village office of each town.

The Directorate of Civil Resistance called for a meeting mandated to all division commanders of the Peasant Battalion.

Furtak of Sochaczew hitched a ride with Scarpek, the commander of Blonie division.

"What do you think; a rising of the peasants?" Scarpek, in his sixties, a former major in the Polish-Soviet War, was trigger happy. Thoughts of war energized him.

"Nothing so dramatic. It has something to do with the quotas. If we comply, the citizens will never make it through the winter."

Scarpek handled the wheel neatly over the ruts carved into the road by the tractor. They were headed for the barn of the Duzat farm.

A large banner was unfurled and hung on the back wall of the barn.

## AS LITTLE—AS LATE—AS BAD AS POSSIBLE

It was the battalion banner and a recent acquisition for the Duzats who had recently become involved in covert activities. Neighboring farmers had regarded them as possible collaborators. Unlike the majority of farmers, the Duzats appeared to have a good working relationship with the village manager, and they always seemed able meet their quota.

One night, Vitzek appeared at a meeting of the local unit. He had the look of a vanquished man. His son, a member of Civil Resistance, was gunned down during a foolish escapade of the boy scouts, of which Felix held no part. Maintaining quotas to keep his family safe was no longer his priority. Was it vengeance, or had Vitzek arrived at a new perception?

The General Government was capable of senseless violence. In time, everyone would be killed or maimed. Vitzek would spend his last breath honoring Felix' diligence to the cause of an independent Poland. The cloak of complicity still hovered over the Duzat farm; the Germans had no reason to suspect them, so the clandestine meeting could be conducted in relative safety.

The Chief Delegate and Virski arrived in separate vehicles. The order of authority must be maintained. In the event of an arrest or an assassination of the chief delegate, Virski would take command.

Jankowski addressed the farmers, "We must move quickly and expeditiously on the destruction of the quota lists. Gentlemen, it is incumbent upon you to round up the unit commanders of your region and inform them of our upcoming disturbance, Operation Quota. It is imperative that procedures be followed explicitly. All of the village offices of a region must be stormed at the same time and the documents burned. The precise timing is vital to your safety. The Nazis will not catch wind of it in time to dispatch gendarmes or remove the documents to a safe place."

Vitzek called out, "What about the land deeds? If they get burned, we have no title to the land."

This was unanticipated. The two officers looked to one another for a creditable reply. The Chief Delegate took it up. "You have a valid point there." He sat back in his chair and tempeled his fingers to his lips.

The audience grew restless.

"Then you must be careful not to destroy any registry records that offer legal rights to the peasants," he continued in an effort to stall.

Scarpek called out, "You talk about time! How much time will be spent trying to locate these registries, and how much time will be spent looking for the quota documents?"

Virski, veteran of sabotage and disturbance replied. "Select a spy, man or woman, to go to the office and request to see the documents for the land. That way you should know exactly which cabinet or box contains the registry. You could do the same to ascertain where the quota files are kept. Send someone in with a grievance about their quota totals or have them ask for a duplicate copy for the one that they misplaced."

"What if the quota files are secured and we can't have access to them."

Chief Delegate did not hesitate, "Burn the building!"

He looked out at the audience, "Furtak, Sochaczew will be first. Meet with your unit commanders and go over plans and logistics. When you have your operation in order, get back to me so we can coordinate the data."

# CHAPTER 38

Michal followed the streets he had walked with Kaminski. Leaves were turning colors on the trees that graced the ill-kempt neighborhoods of Czerniakow. The chirping of birds was the only clue that life went on; the streets were deserted. The mills and factories, which were still operating, kept most of the population sequestered. Those unemployed were no doubt engaged in other pursuits: scavenging for food or involved in subversive activities.

In the eerie silence, the sound of his heels striking the pavement sent out a warning to any of the inhabitants who might be watching the stranger from behind murky windows. There was no dog to bark or cat to run across his path. Animals required feeding.

Michal's ethos was being put to a test. A lifetime of instinctive reactions to the daily routines and experiences of the law and court procedures were being challenged by an unwanted participation in a milieu with which he was totally unfamiliar. This exploration into unknown territory would no doubt redesign and redefine his character.

He steadied his hand as he inserted the key into the lock. He heard the hum of the exhaust fan. Jerzy was waiting for him.

"Bednarek?"

"Yes." He made his way down the steps.

"I have the type set for the next edition. Kaminski had several editorials prepared, and I could use them for fillers. I have the headline set for the lead article."

Michal read the bold type. QUOTA DOCUMENTS DESTROYED

"What do you expect of me?"

"While Kaminski is doing investigative reporting down south. I need you to cover this story."

Michal dropped onto the one chair. This was incredible.

"The chief delegate has instructed all division commanders of the Peasant Battalion to prepare for an operation that will destroy all the quota documents in the village offices. It will involve one district at a time. It must be carefully timed and executed throughout the district. Sochaczew is the first. You know the division commander?"

A perplexed shake of the head.

"It's Furtak. You know the name?"

"No."

"Do you know Dysthmus?"

"No."

"Forgive me Sir, but what—who—do you know of the underground."

He hit a nerve. A strong uneasy feeling released itself; he felt embarrassed, unworthy.

"Zamski."

"You don't know Dysthmus, but you know Zamski?"

"Please, Jerzy, let's get on with this. What is it you need me to do?"

Jerzy quickly jotted down directions to the hideout in Sochaczew, the contact name—Furtak, and the password that would gain him admission.

"You must get there immediately. The date and the hour is set for the operation. I will contact Furtak and make the appointment. What shall I tell him?"

"I will arrive on the milk train tomorrow. I can meet with him at six-forty-five."

Some divine hand of providence was at play. Michal's usual day at civil court kept his appointment calendar clear for the morning. Working alone on checks and balances was the way he spent those mornings, and there was nothing unusual about a magistrate not showing up for court. No one in Warsaw was in control of their comings and goings. His absence would not send off an alarm.

Janina heard him rattling about in the bathroom and rose to prepare coffee for him. He counted on the caffeine to bring clarity to his mornings.

"Pan, are you up for the day? The rooster hasn't sung yet."

"It's my job to wake him today. Thank you for the coffee, Janina. I'll pick up breakfast on my way."

The rail cars were empty. It was a return trip to Sochaczew after depositing the morning's milk at Central Station. The sun's light was picking up the silhouettes of the buildings that bordered the Vistula. It wasn't often that Michal traveled by rail, and he became a sort of tourist as he watched the sun gaining strength to spread a cover of light on the approaching farmlands.

"Sochaczew!" The conductor's call startled him.

He walked the roads neatly drawn and precisely labeled on Jerzy's map. The village store stood exactly at the spot allocated.

He skipped up the three steps to the porch and entered the shop. A bell attached to the door signaled his presence. The drape that separated the doorframe from the living quarters parted, and the storekeeper strode up to the counter.

"I would love to have some bacon!"

"And when was the last time you had bacon?"

"Before the last pig was rationed."

The man behind the counter was deeply tanned. He looked more like a mountain skier than a farmer.

"Come, Furtak awaits you."

Michal followed him to the back door.

"He's in the shed."

Michal walked down the three steps and set his foot on the narrow path that led to a shed that could very well be a toilet; it wasn't much larger.

He knocked, "Bednarek."

A rough looking man in scruffy overalls opened the door. "Furtak."

A small table set up for checkers with two stools held center stage of a storeroom.

"Have a seat." He neatly coupled two glasses in his hand with a bottle in the other. He was about to pour.

"Please, not for me. It's too early, and I haven't had breakfast."

Furtak set the glasses on the table and put the bottle on the floor.

"One minute." He left Michal sitting at the table to observe the pattern of the previous checker game.

He wasn't gone long. "Tomorrow night, at eleven-thirty, seven village offices will be stormed and pillaged. All the quota documents will be burned. You will need to be there as Kaminski's voice. We cannot miss an issue of Poland's Journal. The Nazis are good at putting two and two together."

Another bit of serendipity. Wednesday's were Leona's class meetings. He would leave her a note, and not have to deal with giving an account of his whereabouts.

The door opened and the storekeeper carried a tray to the table. "Here's the bacon you would love to have. I threw in some eggs and potatoes."

Furtak pushed a glass in front of him and poured a shot. "*Na zdrovia!*"

He introduced the storekeeper. "This is Voychek. Be here at six o'clock tomorrow evening and he will bring you to our village office. You will take part in the operation so you can give a first-hand account for your article."

"But, if I live, how will I get home?"

"You'll spend the night with Voychek. He'll get you to the milk train."

Furtak was about to pour another round of vodka.

Michal put his hand over his glass. One *Na zdrovia* was enough for breakfast.

Furtak threw him a condescending glance and poured another draught for himself. "You'll ride directly to Czerniakow. Poland's Journal is delivered on Thursday, and Jerzy has the entire issue set up in anticipation of your lead article."

# CHAPTER 39

Leona could wait no longer. Dinner was held in the oven, awaiting Michal's arrival. She would dine with him after her class.

"Janina, please tell Pan that I've gone to church, and I'll see him afterwards."

She grabbed her light jacket and pulled the door behind her. She was sure to be late. Irena had left half an hour before. Michal had made no mention of having a late day. She had phoned the office, but there was no answer. Where could he be? Wild imaginings flew past her mind. She caught herself blaming Kaminski. He had a penchant for involving Michal in subversive activity.

She slid past the incoming participants for Father Lipinski's scripture lesson. Revelations was a thing of the past, as was the study of Daniel that followed. Father was now offering Wednesday night scripture lessons based on the Epistles.

Behaving in a subversive manner herself, she eased her way into the alcove behind the statue of St. Joseph. It wouldn't do to have anyone spot her going down to the basement.

She didn't have long to wait. Father's voice rang out in the opening blessing with only a hand-full of people in the front rows. It seemed that those in attendance were the newly integrated *Volksdeutsche*.

She entered her classroom with an uncomfortable feeling of apprehension.

Rihard was in his usual seat. He had not been in attendance since Wiadek's capture. He was busy buzzing in Irena's ear. Perhaps the healing process had taken effect and brought him out of hiding. Irena's gentle smile and affirming nods of her head encouraged him to continue his monologue. Neither of them seemed to be aware of the fact that their professor had entered the room. Was there a romance stirring?

The lesson at hand kept her focused, until she heard the stirring of the people in the chapel overhead. It was an early dismissal; no doubt due to the small gathering. Her angst returned and she had the students leave at intervals of two to three minutes apart.

"Do not linger about the church but go directly home. There is always tomorrow to visit with your friends."

The unusual dismissal alerted the students to some possible danger. Warning signals, no matter how ambiguous were instinctively followed by all Warszawians.

When the last student was out the door, Leona grabbed her jacket and book-bag. She flicked off the light and locked the door behind her.

There was a dim light in the hall, and she was startled when she found a strange man standing there.

She let out a gasp and covered her mouth to prevent a shriek.

"Good evening, Pani. I'm sorry if I frightened you."

He was a tall man with broad shoulders. His cap hid his head and most of his face; from the little was revealed, she judged him to be about sixty years old.

"This is my first time to visit this church, and I was anxious to look at the foundation of this magnificent building."

She made an effort to appear nonchalant. "Yes."

"A relative of mine recommended the lessons. He has been coming from the beginning. Father is now in Epistles, Corinthians. I am sorry I missed Romans, my favorite. *And we know that in all things, God works for the good.*" He smiled.

There was a definite German accent. His quote from the bible was disarming.

A smile returned, "Yes."

"And you, Pani; why are you down here in the catacombs?"

An immediate angst, a fumbling for a credible lie.

"A youth group."

"You teach a youth group?"

Teach? Verboten!

"No, ahh, we are preparing a pageant for the feast of Our Lady."

"I shall try to be in attendance." A slight bow of the head.

"Now may I see you out the door? Curfew is almost upon us."

The adrenaline in her system energized her walk home and she was at her door within minutes.

Irena was in the living room, looking over her notes of the evening. "Where is Tata? I don't think he is home."

She dropped her book-bag, without responding to the question, and went directly to his office. She switched on the light and caught sight of a large slip of paper attached to the lamp on his desk.

**Leona, Dear,**

**Please forgive me. I was invited to attend a client's board of director's meeting out of town. It was a last-minute decision.**

**I will be home safe and sound tomorrow at my usual time.**

**I shall miss you terribly. Let's celebrate tomorrow, and dine out, just the two of us.**

**You choose the venue,**
**Michal**

With the note still in her hand, she flopped into the chair. Unprecedented. She was unable to grasp the significance of the situation.

She went into the dining room and poured a tumbler of vodka. She took a gulp and carried it the table by her chair in the living room. The evening's events bustled through her mind. Who was the stranger she encountered in the basement? Was the underground class in jeopardy? The vodka gradually released the stress she had gathered. Where was Michal? She began to relax. She dozed off with the stranger's remark echoing as a final prayer.

*"And we know that in all things, God works for the good."*

# CHAPTER 40

Michal's briefcase held the fabricated balance sheet of a non-existent large farm in the Sochaczew district; some fake receipts for the purchase of tools and equipment, and a change of underwear; in the off chance that a railroad officer would search the contents for contraband.

The second walk to the store was less stressful. The ground was cooling from the autumn sun, a soft breeze rustled the leaves of the trees, and the air held the fragrance of fall. All of this went unnoticed. The grime and provocation of Warsaw and the musty smell of the courtroom was the environment where he felt most comfortable. He was an alien visiting the village, and a novice at gathering information for a news article. What was he doing here?

Voychek called out from the porch, "Bednarek, you're early." He closed the store and hitched up the mule while his passenger climbed aboard the wagon.

"You will have supper with Furtak. You'll stay with him until we rendezvous."

Oats and barley were ripe for harvest, and there were acres of the grain to be cut. The apples in the orchard were being plucked, and those trees waiting for pickers were bulging with fruit. Somewhere out there, the Furtaks were cutting and picking. It was up to Bednarek to find them. He left the briefcase, his hat, and suit jacket on the porch and set out in the direction of the noise of a distant tractor.

"Bednarek!" Furtak's wide brimmed straw hat cast a shadow on his sweaty face. He did not look happy. "We work until dusk. Go back to the house and wait on the porch, until we finish."

Janina's culinary eye would be green with envy. A great bowl of fresh picked fruit sat at the center, loaves of dark bread filled a basket, mounds of potatoes, and bowls of vegetables covered with butter clustered around two roasted chickens and a baked ham. In Warsaw, the tables were bare.

Furtak, his wife Bianca, and their two strapping daughters sat in the chairs around him. Both their sons were in the Home Army, stationed in the forest.

"This is Bednarek," Furtak announced in his gruff voice. A look of recognition mingled with a certain expectancy from the women. "He is writing a story for Kaminski's Journal."

"We know all about you," Bianca grinned, "Zygmunt spoke of you often."

Her comment, and the grin that went along with it, could mean anything. Should he feel flattered or chagrined?

"You brought work clothes?" Furtak wanted to know.

A blank stare.

"You can't go in those church clothes. This is dirty work!"

His daughter, Olga, loaned him a pair of overalls, Bianca brought him a gray work shirt.

The walk to the barn was silent. The full meal needed digesting, so did their thoughts. Many things could go wrong. Driving the country roads after curfew could invite a disaster. Precise timing was another factor; a stalled engine, a flat tire, could throw them off schedule. Furtak had all of this and the careful stowing of munitions on his mind.

Michal suffered a moment of primal angst. What if he lost his life?

They loaded the truck with cans of petrol, guns, ammunition, and grenades. Michal was vividly alive in the present moment. The law, the office, home, all ceased to exist as he took on this new persona. He was an insurgent with no other thought than to wage war, if necessary, to stay alive.

"It's eleven-ten, we roll."

Michal held a flashlight out his window for Furtak to see the road ahead; the muscles of his arm straining to keep it focused on the road. Headlights sent a broad beam of light onto country roads. There was a remote chance that someone might notice their approach and report the after-curfew activity.

Another truck was parked in front of a two-story building that was once a farm house. The office equipment and the official documents of the community were securely locked inside.

"This is Piotrek... Bednarek."

The old farmer offered a hand. "Good luck!"

An appreciative smile.

One swift stroke of an axe unlocked the door. Piotrek pointed out the cabinet that contained the local quota requirements of those who farmed the land. Furtak pulled out the drawers. Piotrek and Michal dumped the contents on the ground outside.

"We don't want to destroy the building."

Piotrek and Furtak poured the petrol. Michal observed the process as Furtak struck the match to ignite the pile. The three of them watched as the fire consumed the documents. Sparks lifted the ash debris into the air. When there was nothing but dying embers, they drove away.

The unit commanders convened at Furtak's barn to give their report. Poland's Journal had to have an article for Thursday's issue. Michal's report would scoop the *Nowy Kourier*.

The operation had been a success. Procedures were followed to the letter at each office. There was only one hitch, reported by unit commander, Bazyl.

"We were still dumping paper on the pile when we heard a motor. We emptied the drawers and we saw the headlights. We ran to our truck. Vitzek was last; he was the one to dump the petrol. Vitzek threw the match and someone, a sharp shooter, shot from the car before it pulled to a stop. Vitzek fell on top the flames. We opened fire, just as the gendarmes piled out of the car. One of them fell. We were able to cover Fredryk while he pulled his brother from the blaze, we helped to drag him to his truck. We took off. We don't know how the Duzat boys are."

"So, you report operation success, with casualties of one gendarme and one peasant?" Furtak glanced Michal's way. Was he writing copy?

He left the train at Center Station and took the tram to Czerniakow with the outline re-arranging itself in his head.

The little yellow light in the living room was enough to show him the basement door. He smelled the aroma of barley coffee; a welcoming gesture?

"Jerzy?"

He made an appearance at the foot of the stair. "How did it go?"

"Very well. I have the outline jotted in note form. It won't take long for me to write the article for you."

"Were there any casualties?"

"One gendarme and one battalion man."

"Gendarmes? Did someone report the operation?"

"Bazyl didn't seem to think so. He thought it was just a routine surveillance check, and the gendarmes got lucky."

"Did either or both die?"

"We don't know. I shall write that up ambiguously."

"Would you like some coffee?"

A wrinkled nose, but "Yes, something hot, if not stimulating."

"Well, there's the typewriter, I'll pour you a cup."

"I don't type."

Jerzy snatched the notepad from his hand. "Really Bednarek, you'd better get your ass together. I'm not going to do everything for you. I operate the hand press. Everything else is up to you."

Michal lowered his head over the cup in his hand, "I understand."

"Did you get the name of the battalion man?"

"Vitzek Duzat. Here, it's in my notes."

He took the notepad. "They'll be found out. The Nazis are brutal on collaborators that turn on them."

"Were they collaborators?"

"Only to the degree that they constantly maintained their quota and were agreeable to the manager and his officers."

Michal stacked the copies and bundled them for delivery; his contribution to his first edition. The two of them came up with the final line for the article.

"It will take months for the General Government to sort out the required quotas for each individual farm. The documents and the duplicates were burned."

Within the next week, all the offices within the Lowitsch District had been ransacked, with casualties on both sides. Strangely, the odds were in favor of the Peasant Battalion. Furtak kept Michal apprised, and Poland's Journal met its deadline.

# CHAPTER 41

Dietrich Weisner, manager of quotas in Sochaczew, arrived at S.S. headquarters on Szucha Street precisely on time for a meeting to discuss the debacle at the village offices. The court proceedings were an important step in the process of transferring the land deed.

The wounded gendarme had died in the hospital. The bullet that was directed at his heart found its mark a minute distance below its target.

His accompanying officer, Behrman, the driver, was called to testify.

"I recognized them immediately, even before Schwartz shot at them. It was the Duzat brothers. The older one was hit and fell face-down on the pile of burning documents. The younger one pulled him out of the fire and carried him off with the help of two other men. I'm sorry, Sir, but I was too intent on trying to fire at the brother to notice the other men. I could not identify them."

It wasn't necessary. The Gestapo had a target.

Vitzek Duzat was carried into the barn. It was an easy exchange from truck to level ground. The four field hands who helped in the process could have easily made it through to the porch and house, but their passenger was in too much pain. Vodka was no help. Fredryk tried to spoon some into his mouth, but Vitzek coughed and sputtered, unable to swallow. The four hefty farmers, men who had dealt with muck and grime all their lives found it difficult to look at the charred skin on his face.

Fredryk remembered how plump and rosy that face was as a child. As the elder brother, Vitzek tried in vain to exercise seniority over him, to no avail. However, it was Vitzek that he turned to whenever his curiosity led him into trouble; the protector whom he never thought to thank, because he took him for granted. Vitzek, the little father, always organizing and getting the job done. The urgency to keep his brother alive was his only thought.

The women entered the barn and reacted wildly. It was during their shrieks and prayers that Vitzek's spirit slowly passed away from the barn, from the fields, from Poland.

It was the morning of Felix' birthday.

Five black autos, bearing the dreaded crooked cross, pulled into the Duzat driveway. Fredryk walked toward the vehicles in a futile effort to delay the entourage.

"Halt!" They piled out of the cars. Two officers raced to Fredryk and cuffed his hands behind his back. German commands were issued and were followed with compliant replies of, "Ya!"

The officer in command, Lieutenant Mueller demanded, "Where is your brother?"

"He's in the field."

All the Duzats were in the field. They had just buried Vitzek. The women heard the approaching vehicles and the German commands and decided to remain in the fields. They separated and found places to hide.

Nine Gestapo officers rushed into the fields to hunt their prey. The lieutenant and two privates remained behind with Fredryk, in order to guard their bound prisoner.

The game of hide and seek did not last long. Matcha was pushed along the road to the house. And the interrogation process began. Rifle butts and clubs drew welts and blood. Matcha collapsed from a blow to the back of her head.

Fredryk's head lolled on his chest; he was dazed from the brutal beating he had endured.

Ludwiga and Halina had taken separate routes to the barn.

Ludwiga pulled the rifle from the shelf over the tools and cautiously made her way back to the house. She swallowed hard when she saw the tactics being used on her son. She knelt down to position the rifle on the porch rail; she steadied the site. Two brown shirts hit the ground. A German bullet entered Ludwiga's chest, another caught her in the head as she dropped to the ground. Fredryk managed to rise from his seat in reaction to the scene, and a final rifle blow split his temple. Matcha never regained consciousness; death offered a peaceful release from further torturous interrogation tactics.

Halina was found lying on the floor of the barn, a malevolent smile on her face. As the soldiers approached the barn, she remembered having seen Felix hide something in the box he kept in a crevice of the wall. Her mother's curiosity prompted her to inspect the contents at her first opportunity. Buried in the slips of paper was a rubbery capsule. She made no mention of it, but she prayed that Felix would never be caught in a situation that would require him to use the pill. It was conveniently left in the box for her.

Fall harvesting was in its vital frenzied stages. The crops had to be stored as soon as possible before the rainy season.

The SS were conducting a harvest of their own. Roundups of innocent victims had increased. Within three days one-hundred citizens were shot. Retribution was running rampant.

The Duzat farm became the possession of the German General Government. Dietrich Weisner and his men would complete the harvest and send the produce on its way to Berlin. This was small compensation for the loss of quota records.

# CHAPTER 42

The usual bustle during the lunch hour was once more under the cool direction of Anna, the hostess. She set the relaxed pace of the dining room with her inimitable grace and personal attention to the patrons and the staff of the Nectar.

Pola was serving two tables, when the handsome young Nazi Lieutenant entered the foyer and waved in her direction. She felt her heart flutter in anticipation of waiting on him, while she coyly fended off his advances. Without thinking, she moved in front of her empty table in preparation for his greeting.

Anna approached him, "Good afternoon, Herr Lieutenant. Your fellow officers are already seated. Let me lead you to their table."

The lieutenant looked from Anna to Pola, standing in wait for him. A brief uncertainty marked his countenance, but he turned and dutifully followed Anna.

Pola was disappointed and unsure as to why Anna had re-directed him.

On her way to the kitchen, she passed Mateusz the manager, who beamed a gracious smile her way. "Pola, dear, have you been to the farm this week?"

"No, Pan, I plan to go this Sunday."

She finished taking an order from her next diner and turned to deliver the check to the kitchen. Jusha, the waitress who served the next station walked up to her with a tray.

"Here Pola, I was on my way back when your order came up." She handed her the tray.

"Oh, I'll take that for you." She reached for the check Pola held in her hand. "I'm going back to the kitchen."

This was not your ordinary day at the Nectar. Valek, the bus boy was right behind her customers as soon as they left the table.

She was about to believe that she was dreaming. Herr Schmidt, her usual grumpy diner, appeared in the foyer. Schmidt was a chronic complainer who never missed an opportunity to criticize the food and the service. He had a penchant for revising the dishes he ordered with some peculiar modifications of his own.

He smiled at Anna and was about to precede her down the aisle to his favorite table, when he too was re-directed, this time, to Jusha's section.

The lunch crowd was thinning at the Nectar. Pola took a late order to the kitchen and placed the check on the spindle. She turned to leave as Anna came through the swinging door.

"Pola, would you come with me? Mateusz wants to see you. Jusha will pick up your order."

What could he want with her? She had never felt entirely comfortable with her first boss. Their longest conversation was on her day of hire, during the interview. From then on it was strictly the patter of social conventions, "Good Morning," "Yes Sir." There must have been a complaint. That arrogant German who complained that his steak was overdone.

Anna opened his office door and followed her in.

Mateusz stood up from his seat at the desk. A warm smile and an extended hand pointed to the chair in front of him. "Ah, yes, Pola; how are you my dear?" He brushed aside the newspaper he was reading.

Anna remained standing by her side. Mateusz threw a questioning eye her way, as though he needed her help. She came to his aid. She stooped down beside the chair that Pola sat in. "Pola, these times require so much from us. May the Saints be with us."

Mateusz took over, this was a poor start; a direct approach was needed. He picked up the water glass from the tray on his desk and filled it with vodka.

Pola was no longer concerned about a patron's complaint. She knew the vodka was for her, along with the suggestion that she call on the saints. She braced herself and accepted the glass, which she held in both hands.

Mateusz continued, "Something has occurred at the farm."

Anna put her arm around her shoulder.

She followed an encouragement to drink some vodka with a trembling gulp.

"The Nazis have conducted a retribution program." He dropped down on one knee on the other side of the chair, his arm around her other shoulder."

"Who has been killed?"

Two hands tightened on her forearms; she was rendered immobile between the two of them.

"Pola, the Germans have confiscated the farm. No one has survived."

One agonizing shriek accompanied a numbing of consciousness; the glass of vodka shattered on the floor.

"Anna, get Valek to run for the doctor. We should have had him here at the beginning."

He rushed to the cabinet on the wall for smelling salts.

Anna returned as Pola regained consciousness, weeping convulsively.

Mateusz' direction to "Have another drink," was ignored; the heaving sobs continued.

Dr. Rozak arrived and a hypodermic was administered. Now that the ordeal of announcing the heinous act was over, Mateusz was left without a follow up procedure.

"Call Dysthmus, he'll take her home." Anna took charge.

Mateusz grabbed the phone to dial Schultz Sewing Machine.

"Joseph, can you send a truck to the Nectar? We have an emergency delivery to go."

Dysthmus parked at the delivery door, and hopped out, clipboard under his arm. Valek, the bus boy had been assigned the duty of waiting for him.

"Mateusz wants to see you." He led him to the office.

Pola had been moved to the couch, and Anna had returned to the dining hall.

Dysthmus didn't bother to knock; he'd been summoned.

"Mateusz, you need armored transport of your day's receipts?" His eyes followed the manager's glance toward the couch.

"Oh, my God!" He shot a frantic look at Mateusz, "What happened?"

"Have you seen today's Poland's Journal?" He handed him the paper.

Dysthmus read the bold print of the headline, AFTERMATH OF DISRUPTION. A quick look at the article provided the names of the victims. His dark complexion waned. He shook his head, unable to fully comprehend the words he had just read.

"What have you done to her?"

"Dr. Rozak has given her a sedative. He says it's a light one and she should soon awake. Can you get her home before she comes to? She let out a horrendous scream and I wouldn't want a repeat of that performance."

Dysthmus was not one to act hastily; he weighed the situation, in an effort to make the right decision.

"Dysthmus!"

"I can't take her to the Piantak's. There is little or no activity in that house. She'll give way to depression. I can't take her; there is barely room enough for me."

"Well, you sure as hell can't leave her here!"

"Help me get her into the truck."

Her body was as limp as a rag doll. They lifted her arms and placed them around their shoulders to carry her to the van, where they deposited her on the floor amidst the boxes and packages.

"Someone is going to have to ride back here with her. She'll be terrified if she wakes alone. Where's Anna?"

"I can't let you have Anna. The customers will be curious and maybe even suspicious if she is not here for the dinner hour. I'll get Valek to accompany you, nobody will miss him."

Dysthmus turned the truck onto Marszalowska Street and headed out of town.

As he drove along the thoroughfare he devised a plan. There was only one place to take Pola, Furtak's. They were still harvesting, and she could put in a good day's work with a family she knew well.

At best, this would be a temporary solution. He would arrange his schedule to find a permanent dwelling and prepare for a marriage ceremony to provide his bride with a home of her own.

# CHAPTER 43

The tumbler of vodka, the soft music, and the prayer that was offered on her rosary, had little or no positive effect. Leona tossed and punched her pillow into a soft hollow for her head, to no advantage. She couldn't remember the last time she slept alone. She thought of Piekalkiewicz' daylight abduction from a tram earlier that year. But the chief delegate had not left a note behind.

The encounter with the stranger had taken a hold on her mind and she felt his eerie presence invading the fitful dreams that occurred when she was able to doze off. She remembered that she felt threatened by his overbearing physical appearance; however, his demeanor was cordial, even gentle. Was his quote from the bible used to assuage her obvious discomfort? She was sure he was German. His Polish was perfect, but she detected a slight German accent. Was he a Nazi? Had Wiadek's arrest opened the door to an investigation that would lead to the uncovering of the history class?

She spent the morning going over the student's journals. There was a gentle irony in the fact that she had learned more of her students through this exercise than they had learned from the entire course. Each one of them handled the issues of occupation from their own inimitable perception. It was easy to identify the fragile ones. The sensitive souls, who would not be able to stand up under German oppression.

Rihard was one of the fragile ones who seemed to have gained a toughness, a shield to guard his artistic nature within a resiliency that might prove beneficial; if the need arose.

She was interrupted from her musings by the sound of the door closing. Michal's greeting to Janina sent a shiver of delight through her body; she sprang from her chair and ran into the hall.

"Where is Pani?"

"Michal!" she fell upon him and pressed into his arms before he could lay down his briefcase.

"What's this? I haven't had a greeting like this since our courtship."

She hung onto his kiss and stayed comfortably tucked in his embrace.

"I shall have to make more of these overnight trips."

A playful smack on his cheek. "Don't try it again, or I too shall have to take mysterious overnight trips."

Leona tugged at his hand and led him down the hall to her study.

"Now, tell me, what have you been up to?"

"It's nothing, really. One of my clients wanted me to observe the meeting of his board of directors in Crakow. It was a last-minute offer, and I didn't have time to notify you before the train left." The ordeal over, he relaxed in his chair, surprised at how easily she accepted this report. He knew he had little skill at lying. Something must be bothering her.

"What's been going on with you? You look a little peaked."

Janina interrupted before she could respond, "Are you ready for dinner?"

Irena made it home in time to wash up before the first course was served, totally unaware that her father had not been at home and in his bed the night before. Leona opted to spin the conversation in a direction that would avoid mentioning anything on toward that might alarm her daughter.

"Rihard has returned to class, after a respectful absence. Apparently, he was very much affected by Adam's capture and execution."

"Oh, he has not been indulging in respectful grief, Mama. He is involved in intrigue."

Michal scoffed, "Intrigue?"

"Yes, Tata. He is involved in the clandestine breaking and entering of the Royal Castle, with that henchman who served Professor Wiadek."

Michal, again, "Henchman?"

"Rihard would not give me his name. He only refers to him as the one who aided the professor in sequestering the city plans."

Leona readjusted her assessment of the young man. "I remember the first time I met Rihard, he mentioned his boyhood fascination with the castle." She gave an understanding nod. It made perfect sense. The boy had a consuming interest in architecture, he loved the castle, and he idolized Professor Wiadek.

Michal's interest peaked, "Please explain, "breaking and entering." What does that mean?"

"The project is on-going and was begun some time ago. This team that Rihard is involved with surreptitiously enters the castle, on an infrequent basis. They must have a key."

"And perhaps, someone working along with them from the inside." Michal interrupted.

"That seems plausible." Leona added.

"Yes, that may very well be the situation. Anyway, they are slowly gathering slips of wall paper, fragments of fabric, from the chairs and drapes, as well as dish and glass patterns and actual furnishings. They anticipate a total restoration of the Castle once the war is ended."

Leona shook her head, an appreciative smile played on her lips. "I wish them every success. Who would have believed the little book-worm would grow into such a valiant partisan?"

After the meal, the Bednareks took to their living room chairs for soft music and sherry. Irena's friend, Dora called and the two of them ran out for a coffee before curfew.

"Michal, I must admit, I'm proud to see my fledgling students growing in courage and loyalty to Poland, but I have a growing concern about their future safety in the church basement."

"There is something concerning you, Leona. What is it?"

"It seems the recent Nazi atrocities on the key citizens of Warsaw and the government officials have had a frightening effect on the parishioners. I have watched the attendance of Father's lectures drastically dwindle. The very inception of the scripture lessons was based on our attempt to devise a weekly population as a cover for the students slipping into the basement to attend class. The small number currently participating in the lectures may throw the focus on the young adults coming on Wednesday who do not join in the assembly. The lack of a reliable cover-up may send up a red-flag."

Michal nodded his head, "This has the potential to jeopardize your class."

"Exactly. Last night, after I locked up and was on my way to the staircase, I came upon a stranger. I hesitate to use the word, lurking, but I was frightened by his appearance." She paused to gain some control before continuing.

He encouraged her to move on. "What did he look like?"

"Strong, and big"

That could mean anything in a size larger than five-foot, three inches. He needed more information.

"What did he say?"

"He said it was his first time in the church and he was interested in examining the foundation. A relative of his had suggested the scriptural lecture."

"Was there something threatening in his demeanor?"

"Not really. I may have overreacted. He asked me what I was doing in the basement. The Angel of the Lord was with me, and I had the presence of mind to make up a story. I told him I was rehearsing a group of students for a pageant for the feast of Our Lady."

She began to feel foolish. On hearing the story unfold as she spoke it to Michal, there didn't seem to be any reason to jump to conclusions.

"You will have to be up front with Father Jan. If this is a dangerous situation, it places the church in jeopardy as well."

She nodded to acknowledge the practicality of his remark. "I'll invite him to brunch after mass, tomorrow. I'm most anxious to know how he will handle this situation." With her concerns out of the way, it was time to grill Michal.

"And now, Michal, just what were you doing last night. I know when you are brushing me off with an untruth. For a lawyer, you're not very good at lying."

He had intended to tell her the truth. It seemed totally dishonorable to hide the fact that he was engaged in active insurgency. However,

Irena's report of Rihard's activities at the castle, along with Leona's fear that her underground class might be uncovered was enough subversive activity for one family to be considering. He would keep his new position as a journalist a secret. For a while, at least.

"No, Leona. That is the truth. I'm uncomfortable revealing my out-of-town visit, because there is a possibility, that with the business growing as it is, my traveling may become a matter of routine, and I know that displeases you."

She stared blankly at him. What was going to happen to them? She was no good at dealing with separation, no matter how short the interval.

# CHAPTER 44

At Home Army headquarters in Warsaw, General Bor reviewed the current issues. There was good news, and bad.

By the fall of 1943, the Germans were suffering huge losses. Hitler's pomposity was losing its power, like a hot air balloon being bought down to the ground. The severe loss of military life in Stalingrad took its toll. The German citizens were beginning to doubt the hyperbole being fed to them by the military propaganda machine. Protestors were rising in Germany's major cities. Security Police found it difficult to keep in check the anti-Nazi handouts that were accumulating in public places. The text of the leaflets targeted the current battles being lost and the cost of lives and ammunition, to say nothing of the ground being surrendered.

The historic battle of Kursk, July 5 to 23, 1943, the largest tank battle to take place, was won at a ratio of three Soviet casualties to one German. However, the Russians were able to re-coop their losses; the Germans could not.

Hitler's machine was breaking down.

This was the good news that bolstered General Bor's resolve. On the dark side was the abrupt cessation of airdrops into Poland by the Western Allies. The government in exile was told that it had become technically unfeasible. There was no mention about when they might resume.

Meanwhile, Soviet General Rokossovsky's Sixty-Ninth Red Army was racing toward the Vistula River of Poland.

Michal had an afternoon appointment with Jerzy in Czerniakow. He slid his key into the lock and closed the door behind him. He could hear voices coming from the basement. He recognized Jerzy's voice and another unfamiliar, robust male voice.

He called down, to test the waters.

"Come Michal, we've been waiting for you."

Jerzy was at work at the typesetter. A large, imposing man in Nazi uniform sat at the desk.

"Michal, Meet my uncle."

The man stood up and extended his hand, "Hienrick Gruber," he announced. The uniform and his size were intimidating, yet his smile was warm and seemed genuine.

"Michal Bednarek." He said no more, waiting for some forthcoming reliable information.

"My uniform concerns you."

"Yes, it does."

Jerzy intervened, "Uncle Hienrick is commander of a secret cell of ethnic Germans from Lodz."

"Ethnic Germans who are involved in diversionary and disruptive action against the Nazi regime." Herr Gruber qualified the statement.

Michal was befuddled He shook his head and took a seat. He wanted much more information and certainly some clarification.

Hienrick rested his elbows on the desk and leaned forward.

"I am a native of Lodz, which has always had a large population of Germans, most of whom are loyal to Hitler and eager to inform on any one of their Polish neighbors."

Michal nodded; he knew the reputation of that city. The secret state was unable to maintain a commander there. Some were murdered, others were informed on by the local Germans. The inevitable outcome was death, by one means or another.

"When the dust settled after the blitzkrieg, and the occupation took hold of Poland, I was instructed, by the Home Army, to declare myself an ethnic German and sign up with the NSDAP."

He unfolded his wallet and produced his card, which validated his official good standing in the Nazi organization.

"Uncle Hienrick is a foreman in a boot factory."

"Yes, we maintain the quota and quality for boots for the Wehrmacht and the Luftwaffe."

He smiled broadly, "I have known these Germans, members of the secret cell, all my life. I trust them with my life, as do they with me."

He stood up to model his uniform. "Occasionally, I wear this outfit to give credence to an on toward activity. I wear it today to authenticate this house as an official residence of a Nazi."

Michal smiled weakly and nodded his head.

Jerzy laid down the palette of letters he held in his hand and moved to the desk, to review his calendar.

"Are you free to meet me tomorrow, at Malakowski Square?" he waited for an affirmative nod. "From there, I will escort you to K-Division Headquarters to introduce you to Kumor. I will be there at precisely three o'clock."

"Very well."

Uncle Hienrick spoke up. "Jerzy tells me that your beautiful wife is engaged in the underground activity of the Flying University."

"Yes." The reply carried an obvious note of caution.

"Please inform her that we are guarding her back. I have embedded two members from my cell, who are currently living in Warsaw, to absorb the scripture lessons of Father Lipinski. They will look after her and sort out any suspicious behaviors that might indicate someone has infiltrated the group as a spy and might uncover the secret basement classes. My men are very involved with the study in Epistles."

This was too much; Michal didn't like mysteries, "I don't understand..."

Gruber stood from his chair and delivered an existing bow.

"Please send my greetings to the lovely Pani Bednarek, tell her "... *we know that in all things, God works for the good."*

Michal selected a soft sonata for the turntable and sat next to Leona on the settee. He watched as she sipped her brandy before he made his announcement.

"By the way, Love, I know the identity of the mysterious stranger from the church basement," his lips spread to display a crafty smile.

She snapped to attention, "Who is he?"

"Did he quote to you from Romans?"

She froze. Was her husband playing the part of an Oracle? She parroted, *"And we know that in all things, God works together for the good."*

"He's a friend of Kaminski's. I mentioned your encounter in the basement and he set up a meeting with this Heinrich Gruber, the leader of a cell of partisans. Gruber has taken an interest in Father's Scripture lessons and has employed two of his agents to maintain surveillance on the meetings in the event a spy should slip in to jeopardize the church as well as your covert classes. Kaminski has your back covered."

# CHAPTER 45

Michal anticipated his upcoming meeting with Kumor with awe and a little dread. The man was an icon of subversive activity.

Vladyslav Petrovski, nom de geurre, Kumor, was Grot-Rowecki's right hand man. Taller than Grot, and leaner, an athletic type. His facial features were irregular and rugged; there was a slight scar on his left cheek. He fought on the opposite side of Grot during the Polish-Soviet War of 1919.

Both men had been incarcerated in their youth. Kumor was arrested by the Bolsheviks in 1918 and conscripted into the Red Army, where he was forced to fight against Marshal Pilsudski. During his internment, he managed to ferret out Soviet military secrets, which he trafficked to the Polish Military Attaché. Fortunately, he was able to escape Russia before he had to answer to espionage charges. He fled to Poland, in 1921, where he joined the Polish Army, and served under General Rowecki. Once the Home Army was established, Grot appointed him to command K-Division, the intelligence unit in Warsaw and the surrounding suburbs.

Michal made his way down the street leading into Malachowski Square, the appointed meeting place. He listened intently for any sounds he could hear over his own footsteps as he walked about the city. It was as though he had sprouted antennae and could feel if someone was tracking him, either by motor vehicle or walking at a distance behind him. He was developing an instinct for survival.

His trek to the square was uneventful. The sun was shining, and the autumn weather was unseasonably warm. For such a pleasant day, there were markedly few people in the square.

Kaminski had told Michal that covert meetings worked best in the open. This bit of sage advice did much to add to his confidence. He selected a bench in the center of the park and sat down, seemingly relaxed and unconcerned. He lit a cigarette and waited for Jerzy to introduce him to the master of intrigue.

Presently, a tall, rugged looking man strolled by. Tobacco pouch in hand, he deftly filled the bowl of his pipe. He stopped in front of the bench and did a cursory search through his pockets. He mumbled something under his breath and then looked over at Michal.

"Please, I seem to be out of matches; could you give me a light?"

Michal obliged and handed him a book of matches. He struck the match along the wooden arm of the bench and puffed on the stem until the tobacco achieved a bright orange glow. He handed the matches back.

"No need, I have others and you are without."

He smiled graciously and took a seat next to him.

He puffed on his pipe and looked out toward the street. "Jerzy is unable to meet with you. Since it is important that we work with one another, I have come directly to you."

Without adjusting his gaze, "I am Kumor."

Kumor was no push-over. He hadn't spent twenty years of his life in intrigue to accept anyone on at face value.

During the meeting at Malakowski Square, he conducted his own interview. In the course of the conversation, he obtained the names of important partisans with whom Michael was involved. Later he contacted the Honorable Judge Peter Butkowski, Prosecuting Attorney Albert Pierski, and Peasant Battalion unit commander Furtak. The references were filed in the first pages of Michal Bednarek's personal dossier.

Kumor contacted Jerzy on the "clearance" of agent Bednarek, and Michal was given the address of headquarters, directions on a secure approach, and a coded knock that identified him for admission. Jerzy obtained an appointment for him, and he was on his way.

Gaining entrance to the hideout went smoothly. Once inside, he was left to deal with his angst. Kumor was involved in a weighty matter, and Michal hung around the waiting area, his anxiety reached a crucial stress level. His daily calendar was considered a legal document by the General Government. The calendar, along with other necessary documents, were periodically examined by the Gestapo in the event that something on toward might reflect suspicious activity by a Pole who was duly licensed to provide services for a German. Michal had elected to set apart two hours in his day for this meeting, which he verified, in writing, as 'ledger documenting.' The next written appointment was with an important Schindlerite.

"Bednarek," Kumor came himself to usher him into his office.

"You need copy for the Journal, and I need to do some propaganda that will boost the morale of the citizens while agitating the Germans. Here's your story."

He hammered out facts and dates without reviewing calendar or notes.

"The Germans continue to suffer great losses. The Reds have entered Chernigov; they are re-claiming their nation, bit by bit. They are less than forty miles from the Dnieper River. Poltava, the important industrial city in Ukraine has been evacuated; the Germans are pulling their forces to cover their losses. Bitter losses in Smolensk drew the Nazis out, and Stalin has reclaimed the city. The fascist government of Mussolini has toppled. Polish forces, under General Anders 2nd Polish Corps, joined the Allies in their march, some ninety miles from Rome."

Michal scribbled legible notes as rapidly as Kumor shot the statements at him. He didn't spend twenty years taking depositions and filing legal contracts to allow a fast talker to out-pace him.

"Finished?" Kumor barked.

A measured nod.

"I look forward to my delivery of the Journal. I will not bother to review your copy. You're an attorney, you know the liable laws. In my court, they will be dealt with severely"

Michal looked at his watch; plenty of time left. He might even indulge in a brief lunchbreak.

Bednarek's secretary, Tessa, had been invited into the clandestine world of subversive journalism. There was no way he could type the report with accuracy and speed. He stashed her finished copy inside the latest *Nowy Kourier* and traveled to Czerniakow to set up the Journal for delivery.

He and Jerzy examined the printed copy. Along with the information gleaned from Kumor, Michal included a busy item on the situation of the Jews in Italy.

"As the Allied troops pushed the Germans northward in Italy, the SS troops rounded up more than one-thousand of the estimated seven-thousand Jews living in Rome. Of that official estimate, some would never be accounted for. Unbeknownst to the Gestapo, more than four-thousand Jews were left hiding in the city. They were given shelter in private homes, convents, and monasteries. Four-hundred and seventy-seven were hidden within the churches, as well as in homes, shops, and abandoned buildings."

"Great job, Michal. Where did you get the information on the Jews in Italy? I know that's not an issue with Kumor."

Michal beamed. "One day, at the Schindler, Kaminski introduced me to a Pan Adamski, manager of the Warsaw Labor Office. I had been very upset about a colleague of mine, who lost his life in the Ghetto Rising. Pan Adamski, a Jew, operating under forged documents, offered me counsel and sympathy. As a result, he and I have become quite friendly."

Jerzy folded his hands behind his head and eased back into his chair; a large smile accompanied his nod of approval.

Finally, the printer had allowed him a positive evaluation.

"Speaking of friends; why don't you come to dinner Jerzy? You pick the night."

# CHAPTER 46

Plump and fifty, Janina had no illusions of romance and dating; the years had passed her by, but she still had an eye to appreciate a good-looking man when she saw one, and tonight's guest certainly filled that bill. Michal entered the foyer in time to catch the look of approval on her face and the seductive shrug of her shoulder. The expanded smile of greeting that he offered his guest was prompted by his observance of Janina's reaction.

"Good evening, Jerzy," he gestured in her direction, "This is our treasured maid, Janina."

"Very pleased to make your acquaintance, Janina."

A blush, a nod, almost a bow, and her hand reached out to receive his hat with a gracious smile.

"So good of you to give up a Sunday evening to dine with us." Michal prepared to usher his guest into the living room.

"Michal, it truly is my pleasure, but we have some work to cover."

Leona entered the foyer during this exchange. Michal was put out for a moment at the wide smile of approval on his wife's face at this total stranger.

"Ah…Jerzy, Pani Bednarek."

She extended her hand and he addressed it with a kiss.

"Pani Bednarek, so very pleased to meet you. The comments I have heard of your beauty do not do you justice."

She offered a coquettish smile, "Please, Jerzy, do address me as Leona."

Michal swallowed his first glass of sherry. Was this a good idea?

They were settled in the living room with canapés, waiting for Irena to make an appearance. She was deliberately delaying her entrance in reaction to her parent's insistence that she be present. Rihard, Stevik, and Dora were spending the evening in town, and she was obligated to stay for dinner with some new friend of her father.

"What is this discussion of work, I heard mentioned?" Leona groped for a topic of conversation.

The dropped comment in the hall, was forgotten by them and they looked to one another for a reply.

Michal, whose head was on the platter, responded. "Oh, yes, Jerzy wanted to discuss ways to put money aside. He is a single man, and every little bit helps."

The off-handed remark left Jerzy perplexed. He accepted Michal's response as a cue. Obviously, Pani Bednarek was not aware of her husband's new responsibility to Poland's Journal.

Irena entered the living room as graciously as possible, under the circumstances. Michal stood from his chair, prompting the guest to do likewise. Jerzy turned to face the newcomer, smile ever ready, and Irena stopped where she was.

Michal rolled his eyes; no one had the right to be this handsome.

Leona looked on, observing every nuance bouncing off the three of them. She could see how easily it would be to write a story based on this mini fraction of a moment.

Jerzy was every bit as impressed with Irena's appearance, as she with his. It was a matter of instant mutual attraction.

Michal fumbled his way through the introductions. Evidently, this was not an old-school chum.

Conversation at table centered on the charismatic young man's family, which he initiated with his casual remark about his uncle, Hienrick Gruber.

"It was my uncle, who first informed me of your beauty, Leona."

A gracious smile, "Yes, Michal was finally able to solve the mystery of the stranger in the church basement. And he is your uncle?"

Irena took her eye off Jerzy to look at her mother. "What stranger, Mama?"

"I didn't want to alarm you, but two weeks ago, after Wednesday evening class, I discovered a stranger," she looked to Jerzy, "I hate to say 'hovering' about the basement. I didn't say anything to you Irena because I had some fears that he might be investigating what goes on in the church basement," she inclined her head toward Jerzy, "obviously, it was his Uncle Hienrich."

Michal filled in the missing element of a solved mystery. "I regularly see Jerzy at the café at lunch, and he informed me that his uncle knew about the underground classes and admired Mama for being so brave. Anyway, Uncle Hienrich has offered to be guardian and watch out for any suspicious character who might be interested in covert activities that might be going on during Father Lipinski's lectures."

"I don't understand; Hienrick Gruber is obviously a German name." Irena waited for an explanation.

"My uncle is from Lodz. You know how populated that city is with Germans. My grandfather was an ethnic German, a prominent lawyer in Lodz, my grandmother, however, was Polish. She was a beautiful woman with a great heart, and she was a marvelous cook. Lucisia was her name; the love she gave us and her faith in God, influenced our behavior and shaped our philosophy. Actually, we had the best of both worlds, the sharp, precision-like intellect of my grandfather, and the soft, spiritual heart of our *Bapca*."

Leona asked, "And from whom did you get your good looks?"

After dinner, the ladies took to their rooms to refresh themselves, before Janina served coffee and dessert.

Michal and Jerzy went to the office, "to discuss Jerzy's finances."

"Michal, I thought we might use, as filler, the story of the German food donations."

The insurgents were constantly sending out communique on official Nazi paper, thanks to Kaminski. They sent out flyers to all the German citizens, instructing them to donate food for wounded German soldiers who were recovering in Warsaw hospitals. In typical German style, the items were listed in exact terms and specific amounts. The donations were to be delivered on a certain date to the German mayor's office.

Michal and Jerzy played with the wording of the incident for an article and came up with a final draft.

We extend our deep appreciation to the beneficent German housewives who delivered food donations for their wounded soldiers to the mayor's office. The confusion caused the Gestapo to intervene and subject all donors to a rigorous interrogation. During this time of concentrated SS questioning, many successful disturbances were completed by partisans. We sincerely apologize for any inconvenience to the well-meaning donors.

"Michal, we won't need clearance on this article from Kumor. There is nothing in it that reveals an on-going disturbance that might go awry because of exposure by the press. From now on, however, it is up to you to deliver copy, of any sensitive nature, to Kumor for his censorship, before we go to press."

"Jerzy, I have an active business to run; I can't spend time waiting in line to speak with Kumor. Besides, he's a very brusque individual and I cannot feel comfortable in his presence."

"He is not singling you out, Michal. That is his style. And you don't have to meet with him; he doesn't have time to deal with you. You simply leave the documents in a sealed envelope with his secretary. Only if there is a problem, will you hear from him. After twenty-four hours, you can print."

An agitated shake of the head. "Very well."

"Didn't you tell me that you knew Zamski? He's here in Warsaw, you know."

"No, I didn't. Do you know where he is staying? I'd like to contact him. There was a last message, given to me by Kaminski, which I am eager to follow."

"Peenemunde! No, I don't know where he is, but I'll let you know when I see you tomorrow."

The gentlemen joined the ladies in the living room. Coffee and desert was served, with a Chopin Nocturne to sweeten the background. The ambiance served to stimulate an engaging conversation. Literature, art and music were discussed. Thoughts of war and an oppressive occupying government were relegated to the reality outside the apartment walls.

Janina finished her work in the kitchen and stepped into the living room to bid the company "good night."

Jerzy rose from his chair and took her hand, "Janina, thank you for the lovely meal you prepared. Not since my grandmother have I tasted such perfect *pierogi*, and I really believe your plum cake was better than what I remember." He placed a reverent kiss on the hand he held.

He looked at his watch, "I must be going. I have very much enjoyed this evening. The family atmosphere and the delicious meal made me forget the everyday problems we face." When he took Irena's hand, he held it for a moment, "Irena, I'm aware that you gave up an entertaining evening with friends to accommodate the family with your presence. I am most honored, and if I may, I would like to make it up to you. Would you consider having coffee with me one evening?"

# CHAPTER 47

Jusha waited on the Nazi Lieutenant who was scanning the dining room.

"Where is the blond—Pola?"

"I'll ask the hostess. I'm not privileged to give out information of a personal nature."

She warned Anna before she put his order in the kitchen. Anna and Mateusz put their heads together and came up with what they thought was a plausible story.

Anna stopped by his table, "You inquire about our waitress, Pola? She's gone off to Nowy Tag to marry her sweetheart," She offered a conciliatory smile as she delivered her report.

The Lieutenant wanted to know, "Where is that?"

"Outside of Cracow." Anna responded.

"What is she doing there?"

"Oh, that's where her family is from. We are distantly related. I'm not sure that I ever met her parents."

It took some doing, but Dysthmus talked Mateusz into the use of his provisions truck.

"I've got to see Pola, and I can't use either one of my vehicles. Sochaczew is too hot, right now."

"Dysthmus, I can't lay up my truck. I have to have fresh produce every day."

"That's just it, Mateusz, I'll bring it back well stocked."

He parked the truck in the drive, next to the house, and set out on foot to find the Furtaks. Pola was the first to notice him. A new tan revealed the time she had spent outdoors to plow and pick. Wisps of blonde hair blew up against the bright print bandana that covered her head. Dysthmus ran to meet her. She appeared to be laughing and crying at the same time.

"*Kochanek!*" He yelled out.

Pola said nothing. By the time she reached him she was sobbing, pitiably. He held her close, "There, there, Pola." His attempts to comfort her, seemed to set her off all the more. He put her at arms-length and looked down at her face.

"I risk my life to come to see you, and you cry?"

She gave a weak titter.

"You look strong and healthy. You'd never get a tan like that at the Nectar."

This time a regular giggle. "I'm more suited to farm work."

Furtak called to them. "Dysthmus, one more hour 'til lunch. Stay with us."

"I can't. Mateusz expects a produce delivery for tonight's dinner. Can you supply me with some fresh greens?"

"Sure, I'll get the girls to pack your truck."

Pola clung to him, her arm around his waist.

"What's happening with the Peasant Battalion, Furtak?"

"Nothing. We're lying low. See that wagon over there?" He pointed to a wagon loaded with grain that was standing near the barn. "That grain has been delivered three times, already. I have three separate receipts for its delivery. This week it goes to the black-market bakery, as a reward for the bread they're handing out to the citizens."

"What the German's don't know won't hurt us." He nodded his head in Pola's direction as a cue that he wanted some time alone with her.

"Okay, I go to fill your truck."

Dysthmus tucked his hand under her chin and kissed her lips. "Where is a shady spot; where we can talk?"

Pola took his meaning and led him to a hillock, behind the house, where a grove of plum trees offered some privacy. Dysthmus had no idea how she was faring after the tragedy at the farm. Her usual sassy demeanor was absent.

He took her in his arms and the attraction they felt for one another served as a respite from the weight of an on-going fight for survival on a brutal playing field. They became alive in the moment. It was just the two of them in a timeless float through space.

Dysthmus sat down on the grass and offered a hand for her to join him. He pulled her close and kissed her neck, while he pushed aside her blouse to explore her breast. Pola was demanding in her response, and they were at the edge of total engagement, when Dysthmus pulled away.

"We're not doing this. If something happens, I can't call it an accident. This is no time to be foolish and put you at risk. There's plenty time for love making after we marry."

Pola tried to separate frustration from anticipation. "Dysthmus, you'll marry me?"

"Of course! Every day without you is agony for me. If I don't marry you and provide a safe place for you, I might screw up on an operation, and that would be the end of me."

"So! You marry me to save your skin?"

# CHAPTER 48

In late October 1943, Zamski made it safely back to Warsaw from London with detailed instructions to General Bor.

"The information is to be shared with Chief Delegate Jankowski. I will remain in Warsaw until you have reviewed the message and are ready with a reply."

Radio operations were becoming increasingly difficult to transmit. Longer messages did not often make it through; complicated problems could not be condensed into "telegraph-ese," and there was always the danger that messages could be intercepted.

The message in Zamski's courier pouch would have never accommodated the restrictions of the air waves.

After much discussion, the exile government and Sosnkowski, the Commander in Chief, had come up with a two-part strategy for Operation Tempest. The operation depended, as always, on the western allies establishing a second front on the European continent. Along with the proviso that they would guarantee direct aid and air cover to Home Army insurgents.

In the event the Soviet armies entered Poland before it was liberated, the government issued guidelines based on two different scenarios.

If diplomatic relations with Russia were re-instated, Operation Tempest was to proceed, in collaboration and liaison with the Red Army Should diplomatic relations remain severed, the Home Army was to go ahead with the operation none the less, but Civil Resistance and the armed forces were to return to their underground encampments and await further instruction from London.

General Bor could not agree with the stipulation that the administrative authorities and the armed forces were to go back in hiding after battling the retreating Germans. He found the precept "unfeasible." He would have to meet with Chief Delegate Jankowski of the Secret State.

Jerzy's announcement, during dinner, of Zamski's presence in Warsaw left Michal pondering how he could arrange a meeting with the courier for the latest news from London. Kaminski did tell him that the Stationery Store was a refuge for insurgents traveling through Warsaw. Wasn't Zamski a traveling insurgent?

Zamski's over-all appearance was less than casual, and he hadn't shaved. Michal had difficulty recognizing the man he had last seen in an expensive business suit, topped with an elegant hat. He sat across from Michal with a mug of coffee in his hand. He wore an un-pressed shirt with an open collar. The shirt might be a loaner from Potopski.

There was some mundane banter about the difficulty of getting radio messages safely transmitted, and Michal found the courier's conversational style most engaging. Cloak and dagger work of a courier spy did not seem to hamper the quality of his social skills. He was a very likeable individual.

"Well, as you see, I had no use of the call letters you gave me, in the event I needed you. The Home Army has brought you to Warsaw."

Zamski allowed a wry smile. "I don't know which takes up more of my time, hiking through the mountains of Hungary to get back and forth, or waiting for political issues to be agreed upon, until a dispatch is prepared."

"Have the latest issues been resolved?"

"No. Obviously, there is a disconnect in how the government in London views strategy and the practical view of the administration here, on the ground of occupied Poland,"

"What can you tell me of Peenemunde?"

"I can't. Where did you hear of Peenemunde?"

"Kaminski's last words to me was about the secret weapon factory and the information the two janitors were able to sneak out to London."

"Well, that is no longer top secret. The RAF conducted a raid on the laboratories."

"In August, wasn't it?"

A non-committal nod.

Michal searched for a way to open up the subject. "Was that the end of the experimenting?"

"No, the Nazis have their teeth on a weapon that will forever change warfare as we know it. They will never abandon the project."

"So, they've rebuilt the site?"

"No, Bednarek, I know you're searching. Let me put your curiosity at rest." He held his eyes on Michal. Was he about to bring out a bible to swear on?

"I depend on your holding this information secret, until I give you word."

"Zamski, I'm a professional lawyer. I know the criteria for non-disclosure. You can depend on me in the very same manner you dealt with Kaminski."

"The Germans have begun construction of laboratories in Blizna, in Gmina Ostrow. That's in southeast Poland."

Michal got the connection, Peenemunde—southeast Poland, Kaminski!

"Why there?"

"It's far safer. The territory is outside of the range of allied bombers.

At the end of November, Courier Zamski left Warsaw and headed north for his trek over the Carpathian Mountains to Slovakia and through to Hungary. The trick was to avoid the German frontier patrol on the borders.

In his pouch was the delayed response from Bor. A final resolution had been agreed upon between the commanding general of the Home Army and the chief delegate of Civil Resistance.

General Bor-Komorowski took issue with Commander in Chief Sosnkowski's instructions that covered the event of unsettled diplomatic relations with the Soviet. The C in C's recommendation that the troops of the Home Army should go into hiding after battling the retreating Germans, was antithetic to what was actually going on in the political and military arena of Warsaw. Bor found the proposition of going underground, should the Russian troops approach, unfeasible.

The commanding officer of the Home Army was at variance with the Commander in Chief. He issued orders to all provinces and districts in Poland. All units were to emerge into the open after taking part in operations, in order to establish the existence of the Republic of Poland. He concluded the orders with the proviso that the operation was to engage in battle with only the German troops remaining in Warsaw. There was to be no confrontation with the Russians entering the territory—unless it was a matter of self-defense.

On his visit to London, Chief Delegate Jankowski, upheld General Bor's position. There was no denying the fact that the communist organizations in Poland, with the sophisticated intelligence system of the NKVD, were already apprised of the underground leadership in Poland. What purpose would be served to have the Home Army go back into hiding after doing battle with the retreating Germans?

# CHAPTER 49

Jerzy gave a soft rap on the Bednarek's apartment door. To his surprise, Leona was the one to admit him.

"Good evening Jerzy. You are a bit early. Irena is not quite ready."

He took her hand and kissed it, after which he presented her with a yellow rose. "For the lovely mother."

"How gracious! Come, we'll have a sherry while we wait for your dinner partner."

He followed her into the living room. "Where is Janina, this evening?"

"Oh, she is in the kitchen, preparing our dinner."

"Allow me." He walked over to the bar and poured their drinks.

"Thank you," a smile, somewhat sweeter than need be, "Tell me what is it that you do for a living, Jerzy."

"You mean what does it state on my *Ausbeis*?"

A nod, the smile remained.

"I deliver a newspaper."

"Oh, which one is that?"

"The *Nowy Kourier*."

Irena entered the room with an expectant air about her. She knew there would be a show of approval. The purple color of her dress complemented her complexion; her hair was styled in the latest brush curl, and she carried her height like a model on the runway.

Leona lost her opportunity to question Jerzy about the *Nowy Kourier*.

"Good evening, Jerzy. Has Mama been grilling you about your intentions for the evening?"

Jerzy smiled in appreciation at the boldness of her remark.

"Irena, really!" Leona shifted into the role of a concerned mother. "And where will you be taking my daughter, Jerzy?"

"We dine at the Nectar. After which I will bring her directly home."

"The Nectar? Isn't that a German establishment?"

"They cater to the Germans, but it is definitely a Polish operation."

Irena kissed her mother's forehead, "Please, tell Tata that I'll stop in to see him before I go to bed."

Jerzy took Leona's hand, "I promise you I will behave in every way, the gentleman."

"Thank you."

"Now, may I step into the kitchen to say hello to Janina?"

"Of course, she would be most disappointed if you didn't."

Once outside, on the sidewalk, Irena snickered. "Janina was disappointed when Mama told her that she would be the one to open the door for you. I know that Mama wanted a chance to speak to you alone and find out what she could."

He tucked her hand under his arm, "I suspected as much. I don't blame her; you're her greatest treasure."

Leona poured a tumbler of brandy; she needed it. She had just allowed her daughter to go, un-chaperoned, to a German restaurant, with a man who definitely had a German heritage—and a German uncle. A man who delivers the German propaganda rag, the *Nowy Kourier*.

Anna greeted them and took them to Jusha's table. On the way, diners already involved with their meal smiled and greeted the familiar young man. Those Aryan good looks had made a virtual celebrity of Irena's escort.

"How is it you are so popular?"

"Well, I meet these people in my daily work."

Jushka delivered the menu and waited for their order.

"Irena, shall I order for you? This is typical German fare, and you may not be familiar with the dishes."

She wasn't familiar with the cuisine, but she did enjoy the meal. Perhaps the novelty added to the taste and presentation.

"Jerzy, how do you know my father?"

He was treading on unsettled ground. "He's another one of my customers," was his offhanded reply.

"Ah, here is Jusha, with the dessert menu. What say you to some strudel with ice-cream on the side?"

In the hallway of the apartment, Jerzy took her in his arms. He gently kissed her cheek.

"I should love to come to dinner this Sunday."

# CHAPTER 50

At the time of the Tehran Conference in November 1943, the world could not anticipate the imminent death of the President of the United States in just five short months. It was said that FDR once told Orson Wells, "You and I are the greatest actors in America, today."

The leader of the most powerful nation in the world, arrived in a wheelchair to attend the conference after having traveled seven thousand miles to get there. It was to be his first meeting with the Bolshevik leader of the Soviet Union, Joseph Stalin. He was ill-prepared to deal with the strong-willed dynamism of a man who was so determined to dominate and suppress the natural order of things. Stalin would trample over anything that got in his way.

Churchill was the leader of an empire. He had dealt with many would be conquerors. He had already formed a definite opinion of the rough little peasant who had an engaging manner.

The conference opened with a dinner on the evening of November 29, 1943. It was Churchill's birthday, and a cake had been baked to celebrate the occasion.

Stalin had his agenda well planned. He came to the table with considerable credit at his disposal. The Soviet Army was aggressively driving the Germans out of Russia. In spite of his reputation as a brutal killer, he had a natural charm and wit that he could display in diplomatic situations. At his first meeting with the President of the United States, he paid a compliment to the American worker, stating that their efforts in producing weapons and ships to aid the war effort was indispensable to the United Nations.

After this ingratiating remark, he reverted to his true nature by commenting that the Germans were habitual warmongers. "In order to prevent a third world war, fifty-thousand to one-hundred-thousand German officers should be executed."

Roosevelt was stunned; was this a joke? Not knowing how to react, he quipped, "Maybe forty-nine thousand would be enough?"

Churchill was appalled by Stalin's comment. He denounced the remark as, "the cold-blooded execution of soldiers who fought for their country." He referred to the Moscow Document which stated that only war criminals should be put to trial.

Churchill stormed out of the room.

Stalin took on the role of peacemaker and followed him. He assured the Prime Minister his remark was made in jest. Churchill returned to the table but harbored a feeling of mistrust toward the great bear of Russia. Was Stalin testing the waters?

During the negotiations, Stalin played his trump card, "bargain and manipulate." He already had his bargaining chip, the Soviet victory of the Battle of Kursk; that and Stalingrad were sure to garner the results he had in mind.

Stalin's part of the deal was a commitment to the alliance; the Red Army would launch an offensive attack against the retreating German forces transferring from the Eastern to the Western Front. This battle would coincide with the Western Allies long planned for invasion of France. Operation Overlord, the establishment of a second front, was scheduled for May of 1944.

Britain and the United States were romancing Turkey to enter the war against the Nazis. Their production of chrome was vital to the manufacture of the strong steel needed to build the heavy armor tanks of the Wehrmacht. To shore up any reservations the Turks might have, Stalin volunteered Soviet forces to declare war on Bulgaria, should they decide to turn against Turkey.

Negotiations require compromises. Roosevelt and Churchill were urged by Stalin to recognize the communist government of Marshall

Tito of Yugoslavia as an ally. As an added incentive, Yugoslavia would receive supplies and equipment via airdrops from Britain and the USA.

Stalin then brought out the big guns. The Curzon Line. The Western Allies agreed to a shift of the western border between Poland and Russia. Stalin accepted Churchill's proposal of compromise. For the loss of Poland's marshlands and the city of Lwow in the east to Russia, territory to the west belonging to Germany, would be offered to Poland as compensation.

Stalin's mission was accomplished. He held the territory and the political future of Poland in his hip pocket.

News of the Tehran Conference leaked to the exiled government in London. Although the information was second-hand at best, Commander in Chief General Sosnkowski had his own interpretation of the results. His analytical mind explored the big picture. He was aware of Mikolajczyk's meeting with Anthony Eden, Britain's Foreign Secretary. The fact that the premier had requested Eden's aid in promoting a diplomatic alliance with the Soviets, convinced Sosnkowski that Mikolajczyk and his staff were eager to make concessions to the British to maintain the support of the Western Allies.

The C in C was also apprised of the Allies acceptance of Yugoslavia as an ally. Britain and America were sending arms and ammunitions via parachute drops to aid them in their battle against the Germans.

Chief Delegate Jankowski was in London and Sosnkowski sought him out. "Does it surprise you that the allied air-drops have been dis-continued?"

Jankowski wasn't surprised; he was devastated. "We have been told that technical difficulties involved in the flights are the reason for the end of their support."

"Stalin has informed Churchill and Roosevelt that the Home Army is collaborating with the Nazis. He also accused the underground military of murdering Polish communist partisans."

"Surely the allies can't accept this as truth!"

"No matter. I have spoken to a British officer who told me the Yugoslavs were actively involved in offensive battle against the Nazis, while the Home Army was merely defensive in its activities."

Sosnkowski lit a cigarette with the left-over butt of the one he had just smoked.

"It seems there are no technical difficulties involved with flights over the mountains of Yugoslavia." He drew long and hard on the cigarette.

# CHAPTER 51

Diversion and disruption had eased up—for the time being. The peasants were far too busy with the harvest and maintenance of the buildings and equipment on their farms. After the disaster of the Duzat Farm, it was time for the Peasant Battalion to lie low.

Pola pulled her weight with the housekeeping chores and with the recent harvesting on the Furtak farm. The hard work, the family's bickering and jibes were what she was accustomed to, and in this atmosphere of familiarity, a gradual healing took place.

Dysthmus was happy with the progress she had made; she may never get over the effects of losing everything she held dear, but she was recovering and seemed to be developing a new sense of her personal identity. He visited the farm as frequently as possible, helping with the farm chores whenever he could. There continued to be a demand on his time and service for diversionary activities within the secret state. The Schultz Sewing Machine truck could not be put at risk, and so once again he counted on his resourcefulness.

The Home Army motor pool allowed him the use of a run-down truck that was equipped with lumber slats on three sides of the bed, complete with a tarpaulin cover. Dysthmus was officially in the produce business. His second *Ausbeis* identified him as Marek Gruzek, Purveyor to Restaurants. This enabled him to make at least one delivery a week to the Nectar restaurant with the farm products he hauled from Sochaczew.

Winter was approaching, Furtak and his men did the back-breaking work of harvesting and threshing the grain, shoring up the roofs, and caulking any holes in the barns and sheds. Canning the fruits of the harvest and storing the root vegetables and bacon, was left to the women to ensure that a sufficient food supply was available to carry them through the winter. They were also busy embroidering borders on sheets and pillow cases to be included, along with some kitchen equipment, in a hope chest that Furtak converted from an old linden storage box.

Marek was on hand to help with storing the fodder for the animals over the winter. At the end of the day, Furtak took Marek up the hill into the orchards. Not far from the main barn, sat an old fodder house.

"I'm storing the fodder in the barns this year. I was able to make room. This building sits nice and flat. From the window is a nice view of the plum orchard."

They walked inside. The space within the four walls was empty; there were no dividing walls, there was one small window next to the door.

"This is big enough for a bedroom and kitchen; there's an outhouse a few feet away. I have a good stove for you and the furniture from the boy's room…"

Marek grabbed him for an overwhelming bear hug.

"Thank you, Furtak. You know neither Pola nor I have family. We are adopting the Furtak's to be aunt and uncle to our children."

By the winter of 1943, Kumor realized that the division of diversionary activity was so widespread that casualties were escalating in the ranks of the insurgents. Some of the operations seemed to be ill-planned and wound up sacrificing the safety of the men in their desire for expediency. The operation of subversive tactics had grown tentacles that were reaching everywhere into the field of German operations. Polish workers in the German munitions factories produced dud shells and faulty gun muzzles. Teams of men were organized to rescue prisoners from Pawiak Prison. The usual performance of sabotage activities such as; train derailment, dynamiting bridges, and the burning of official German documents, was constantly disrupting the Nazi agenda.

But now there was an added burden. The Home Army was no longer eligible for aid from the western allies. Air drops had ceased. How were they to plan a national uprising without a reliable source of weaponry? The storehouse in the forest was not only limited, but the environmental ravages over time, had rendered much of the arsenal useless.

The winter of '43-44' appeared increasingly bleak.

# CHAPTER 52

The German garrisons were taking on the spirit of Christmas. There was an undercurrent of frivolity, mostly among the homesick non-commissioned officers, who were being wined and dined by the German citizens of Warsaw. The *Volksdeutsche* and the transient Germans who were involved in the occupation were delighted to invite the young men into their homes to share in the customs and traditions they remembered in the Fatherland.

The roundups of citizens to be shot in the streets had not let up, but each garrison office sported one small *Tannenbaum,* a Christmas tree. In the outlying suburbs, where diversionary activities weren't as intense, here and there a Nativity Scene might be found beneath the tree.

The Poles were following the same precept. Every dwelling, no matter how modest, at least displayed a green wreath or garland. The Secret State conducted the usual subversive actions. For both parties, it was "business as usual," along with a nostalgic note for the season of joy.

Michal had received generous gifts from his wealthy Schindlerites. One of them presented Michal with a hand-knitted scarf, made by his wife. As for his clients, they had ended the year with a surplus of digits in their bank accounts.

It was time for the Bednareks to celebrate.

"Jerzy, is it possible to have Uncle Hienrich dine with us this Christmas?"

"I don't know; I'll ask him. When did you have in mind?"

"Leona insists on celebrating Christmas at church and exclusively with the family. Undoubtedly, she'll choose a Sunday before Christmas. I'll let you know as soon as she and Janina have firmed things up."

The aroma from the kitchen wafted into the hall, welcoming the guests before they knocked on the door. Janina had all burners going, a ham was in the oven; the baked goods were cooled and decorated the day before.

Father Lipinski was the first to arrive at the Bednarek doorstep. He had spent the time and expense to purchase a large box of Swiss chocolates available at one of the bakeries that catered to a German clientele. Uncle Hienrich's contribution was a bottle of cognac.

Janina greeted the guests wearing an evergreen corsage and a large smile.

The apartment was appropriately decorated with garlands draped over the windows. Polish Carols in the background made the ambiance complete.

Canapés and vodka provided a congenial setting for the guests to become acquainted with one another. Father Lipinski opened the festivities with a special Christmas blessing and then started the flow of conversation.

"Leona, I am happy to report that the approaching holiday motivated an enthusiastic desire for many parishioners to join in the scripture lectures."

"That is good news, Father," a quick glance in Hienrick's direction, before she continued. "I hope you can sustain that group; however, I shall be taking a semester hiatus. My current class has fulfilled their requirement for the grade, and I will be looking to start another class."

"Why don't we meet tomorrow afternoon at the center café, for coffee?" Lipinski lowered his head to look over his spectacles while he delivered that benign smile of his.

Jerzy took a sip of his after-dinner cognac, and then made a request. "Leona, will you allow me to select record from your collection?"

She was still harboring thoughts that he might possibly be a spy, but she was not about to permit such thoughts to dampen a holiday dinner.

"Of course, my darling boy. How could I refuse you anything?"

Chopin's Fantaisie in F Minor was right on top of the pile. A favorite of Leona's, it was playing the first night Jerzy came to dinner.

He walked over to Irena's chair and knelt on one knee. An affectionate smile on his face kept her occupied while he dug into his pocket for a small white jewelry box.

"Irena, I have here the ring my grandmother wore. I feel it belongs on your finger. Will you marry me?"

Irena tried to maintain composure. She allowed him to place the ring on her finger. Her response was slow. She knew how much family meant to him. Could she fulfill his expectations?

"Oh, yes, Jerzy," she put her arms around his neck, "I most certainly will!"

Leona rose from her chair; she was unable to maintain composure. In spite of her tears, she felt a tinge of anger. She looked over at Michal, "Did he ask your permission?"

Cognac made the rounds again. The engaged couple decided to take a walk, to be alone. A brief period of silence hovered over the room while the company adjusted to the aftermath of the romantic scene.

Hienrich attempted to fill the void. "I go back to Lodz this evening; tomorrow is another workday, but I have some information that would be of relevance to you, Michal."

Leona and the priest turned their attention to what he had to say.

"Early in November, a unit commander from the Home Army was invited by a Soviet unit commander to discuss the possible co-ordination of forces against the retreating Germans. It is not known if Bor sanctioned the proposed meeting, but the commander showed up at the site in the company of fourteen men from his unit. They have not been seen since."

Leona was shocked by the information, "That is horrific, but why would this be of interest to Michal?"

"It will make good copy for Poland's Journal."

Michal fumbled, "It's nothing to concern you with, Leona. I will explain everything to you after our guests leave."

Just before noon, on Christmas Eve, Michal was treated to an unexpected visit. Kaminski showed up at the office.

"Come, I'll treat you to lunch at the Nectar."

Michal got most of the update of Kaminski's hot story on the walk to the Restaurant.

"The Nazis have moved their rocket operations to Blizna, where it's safer for them to continue, uninterrupted by Allied bombing."

"Have they torn down their laboratory in Peenemunde?"

"No, that operation continues, although I'm certain in a more modified mode."

"How did you discover the whereabouts of the new test site?"

"The Home Army has known about it since construction began in early November."

Kaminski seemed quite amused when Michal told him about Hienrick blowing his cover during a Christmas celebration.

"Zygmunt, you must come home with me this evening. Leona is still quite unsettled in the matter."

"This is Christmas Eve, and I have several invitations that I must honor. One of them is with an engineering friend of my father."

He reached out for a handshake, "Michal, I don't know when, or if, I will see you again. The allies are committed to opening a second front, and if they do, we Poles will be responsible for dealing with the exiting Germans from our country. Meanwhile, I am involved with matters in Blizna, and I depend on you and Jerzy to keep the Journal going. Maintain communication with Virski and Kumor and stay in touch with Hienrick. He's a very resourceful individual. We will continue to work together via radio messages. I'm like the Holy Spirit, I'll never leave you on your own."

Michal tightened his grip on Kaminski's hand. He did not respond, an image of total destruction flashed across his mind's eye. The next year would be the decisive end of the war. Would Poland achieve her long-awaited Independence?

# CHAPTER REFERRENCES

CHAPTER 1:
University Poznan/*Volksdeutsche,* Wikipedia: Poznan
Soviet-German Treaty of '39, Davies page 30, 124; Gilbert page 16
General Stefan Rowecki, brief bio, Wikipedia
No contact upward, Davies 184
Underground Press: Davies page 185, Korbonski page 163

CHAPTER 2:
Pieklakiewicz, Korbonski page 112
Amended strategy for Operation Tempest, Wikipedia: Prelude to
Warsaw Rising
Hostile attitude toward Russia, Davies page 205
Exiled Government, Davies page 34; relocated to London, page 36
Thousands of Russians slaughtered by Stalin, BLOODLANDS by
Timothy Snyder page25

CHAPTER 3:

Airdrops, Bor-Komorowski Pg. 72; from February 15, 1941, 488 flights
brought arms/ammunition aid 64 flights failed to return to Home Base,
24 of the flights were manned by Polish pilots.
Doctor's Prescriptions Korbonski 118
Slave laborers, Davies 106
BBC sign-off tune as cue, Bor-Komorowski page 72

CHAPTER 4:
Cardinal refusing to meet with Frank, Korbonski page 171;
Cardinal's residence near Frank's HQ, Wikipedia Ibid
Role of Clergy, Davies page 186; Korbonski page 170-71
Professor Jan Pieklakiewicz, Korbonski page 112; Lukas page 175
Bible reference: Romans 8:25 NIV
Urgent Labels, Korbonski page 220

CHAPTER 5:

Tavish—Mateusz Rataj, Korbonski page 18
Brigadefuhrer Jurgen Stroop, Davies page 115
Schindlerites, Davies 95

CHAPTER 6:
Contraband food sewn in women's clothes, Korbonski page 221
Quota demands Korbonski 216

CHAPTER 7:
SOA, Korbonski page 187
History of railway disruptions, Bor-Komorowski 39-41
Peasant Battalions, Korbonski 214
Grain quota spill, Korbonski 215
Caloric Intake, Korbonski page 219; Davies 105

CHAPTER 8:
Closing of secondary schools and universities in October 1940, Davies
page 94-95; Wikipedia: Education in Poland during WW II

CHAPTER 9:
Trial of "URGENT" labels, Korbonski 220
Illicit stills, Korbonski page 245
Illegal bakeries in and around Warsaw, Korbonski page 220

CHAPTER 10:
Crypt of Catholic churches for clandestine education classes, Davies 186
Shooting of German soldiers in Nectar, Korbonski 267

CHAPTER 11:
Proper paper products, Nowak page 100
Aaron, based on brief bio in Wikipedia, Henryk Wolinski; Courier from Warsaw by Jan Nowak page 173-74
Zegota, Davies page 200; Wikipedia: Judenrat; Zegota; Jewish Combat Organization
Preparation of Rising, Davies 96-103

CHAPTER 12:
Location of Court House, Nowak page 106; Korbonski 257
Jewish colleague, 258

CHAPTER 13:
Katyn, Korbonski 270; Davies 115; Bor 126; Wikipedia: Katyn Massacre

CHAPTER 14: Recruit, no references

CHAPTER 15:
Polish Division retreating from German forces, Bor 126

CHAPTER 16:
Churchill's SOE, Davies page 8
Goebel's press release re: Katyn, Davies 115
Pro-Soviet majority in British Government, Davies 49
Broken Russian-Polish Non-Aggression Pact 1941, Davies 48
Boycott of German venues, Davies 187
Film of Katyn, Davies 115

CHAPTER 17
Ghetto Rising, Davies 96-103; Bor-Komorowski 95-109; Korbonski 261-63; Wikipedia: Ghetto Rising

CHAPTER 18:
Grey Ranks, Davies 176-7

CHAPTER 19:
Starvation diet, Wikipedia: Nettle Soup; Orache

CHAPTER 20:
Stationery Store, Korbonski 24
Blue Police, Davies 89
Sanctuary, Korbonski 43

CHAPTER 23: Prison
Pawiak Prison, Korbonski 33
Frank's visit, Korbonski 35

CHAPTER 24: Invitations
Tactical shift d/t increased revenue from Warsaw, Davies 87, 114

CHAPTER 26: Architect
Warsaw City Planning and Development, Davies 187

CHAPTER 27:
Secret Courts, Korbonski 124; Davies 198
Process and sentencing, Korbonski 126
Lieutenant Lukorski, Korbonski 130

CHAPTER 30:
Liaison girls, Bor-Komorowski 59-

CHAPTER 32:
Gestapo enter Spiska Street, Bor-Komorowski 139
Capture of Rowecki, Lucas 93
Recovery Team to Spiska Street, Bor Komorowski 141

CHAPTER 33: Black Week
Brief bio of Komorowski, THE SECRET ARMY, Forward by Adam
Komorowski; Davies 31; Wikipedia: Tadeusz Komorowski
Pseudonym "Bor" first appearance, Bor-Komorowski 142
Death of Sikorski, Davies 190; Bor-Komorowski 142; Wikipedia: Death
of Sikorski
Kalkstein, et al, Davies 111; Lukas 93; Wikipedia: Ludwik Kalkstein

CHAPTER 34:
Bor's report, 143
Description of Sosnkowski, Nowak 221
City of Czerniakow, Wikipedia
Packet of information re: Peenemunde, Davies 201
Two POWs [janitors] uncover plans of new weapon, send packet to BI
Wikipedia: Peenemunde, Chapter 3
RAF raid, August 15/16, 1943, Davies 201; Bor-Komorowski 151;
Wikipedia: Peenemunde, Chapter 3
Blizna, Bor-Komorowski 152; Wikipedia Chapter 3
Description Mikolajczyk, Nowak 22

CHAPTER 38: Romans
"All things…, Romans 8:28 NIV

CHAPTER 39: Village Office
Peasant Battalion Banner, Korbonski 214
Burning official documents, Korbonski 217

CHAPTER 42: Bor
German's protest against Nazi war, THE SECOND WORLD WAR—
Martin Gilbert 412
Battle of Kursk, Davies 43; Gilbert 445
C in C's directive/proposal, Bor-Komorowski 174-76; Davies 206;
Nowak 212-13
Bor's variance, Bor-Komorowski 178; Davies 207

Lodz, Nowak 95
Uncle Hienrich—modeled after Anatole, Nowak 95-96

CHAPTER 43: Table Talk
Rihard at Royal Castle, Davies 187

CHAPTER 44: Kumor
C in C's directive/proposal, Bor-Komorowski 174-76; Davie 206; Nowak 212-13
Bor's variance, Bor-Komorowski 178; Davies 207

CHAPTER 45: New Copy
Reds enter Chernigov, Gilbert 463
Stalin reclaimed Smolensk, 463
Poltava, Ukraine, 463
Mussolini toppled, 465
General Anders on route to Rome, 466
Hidden Jews in Italy, Gilbert 467

CHAPTER 50: Tehran
Tehran Conference, Davies 45; Wikipedia: Tehran Conference
Stalin's trump card, Kursk, Wikipedia: Tehran Conference page 3
Turkey involvement, Wikipedia page 3
Recognize Tito in Yugoslavia, Wikipedia page 2
Curzon Line, Davies 63; Wikipedia page 3
C in C Sosnkowski's interpretation, Nowak 212-13

Made in the USA
Middletown, DE
19 March 2022

62908827R00137